BITE THE BULLET

A Novel

JIM WOODS

Thanks for Reading!

Jim Woods

D1528157

For
Jack, Kate, and Kristal

ACKNOWLEDGMENTS

I would like to thank each of these people for a thousand reasons: Anna McKenzie, Kristin Talgø, Katelyn Johnson, Todd Foley, Kent Sanders, Tammy Helfrich, Harris III, Mike Vardy, Chad Jarnagin, and Ben Arment.

Thanks to Jeff Rueger, Nathan Honaker, Joe Cacioppo, and the many members of law enforcement and emergency services that I've spoken with over the years.

Thanks to Danielle of Shelf Life bookstore for your friendship and support. Your love of books and amazing spirit of generosity is contagious! Thanks to Gift too for all of your hard work behind the scenes.

Thank you to everyone who has given me support and encouragement.

Thanks to Kristi Griffith for your help with the cover. I sincerely appreciate it.

I would also like to thank my editor, T.K. Johnson, for her support and many insights.

Special thanks to my family. I love you very much.

"Revenge is simply justice with teeth."
  Simon R. Green

CHAPTER ONE

Sergeant Ryan Malone wanted to scream when reading the headline of the *Chicago Sun-Times*:

"$500,000 in Heroin Confiscated."

He scowled as he cursed under his breath. Then he tucked the paper under his arm and took a sip of coffee. To his right, he saw two tourists posing for a picture in front of the Nike store. He scowled again and climbed into his black Chevy Impala. He saw his reflection in the rearview mirror. His short brown hair was standing up from the wind, and he patted it down with his hand. The stubble on his square-shaped jaw was mostly dark but revealed specks of grey that framed the frown on his face. Malone looked over at his partner, Max. With his lean build, brown Italian leather jacket, and spiked black hair, Max looked more like a rock star than a cop. Max slouched in the passenger seat, blowing a puff of smoke through the cracked window.

"Can't believe this shit. A major bust the day after crime stats are released," Malone said, tossing the newspaper on Max's lap. "This time it's 500 grand in heroin. Some fucking suit is pulling strings to spin stories while the goddamn city is dying."

Max leaned forward in his seat and turned toward Malone.

"People are busy, man. They got jobs, they gotta pay the rent. They're gonna watch football, get drunk, and get laid. Unless you're on the South Side, no one gives a shit what's going on down here. It ain't nothing new. Just some gangs at war with each other and politicians spinning shit to get their asses reelected."

"I'm sick of this goddamn game. The assholes got it rigged. Shit, they just released Ramon Garcia. There's your headline. That bastard's a parasite killing the city."

"Yeah, I know. That asshole never should have got parole."

"You're bumming me out. Making me wanna get a drink," Malone replied.

"Always been this way, you know?" Max said.

"Then what the hell are we doing?"

"Might not look like it, but we're fighting the good fight," Max said with a smile. "Taking down one bad guy at a time."

"Still a bunch of bullshit," Malone grumbled, pulling out onto the street. "Hey, hand me my sunglasses, will ya?"

Max pulled a pair of cheap black sunglasses out of the glove box and gave them to Malone.

"Thanks, it's bright as hell out here today."

"No problem, Johnny Cash."

"Huh? Hell are you talking about?"

"You know other colors exist, right?" Max said as he pointed at Malone's black sunglasses, black leather jacket, black button-down shirt, and dark-colored jeans.

"Whatever, man," Malone laughed. "Why don't you pay attention to the job, eh?"

"You know... since Jerry's put in his papers, maybe we can

get more done," Max said, blowing another puff out the window. "Just don't rock the boat too much and piss everyone off."

"Yeah, I'll leave that one to you," Malone said with a laugh.

"We gotta start looking out for ourselves. Bet half the force is on the take."

"Probably more than that. But it ain't about the money. I just wanna see some fucking progress. 'War on Drugs' my ass."

"I hear ya. Maybe there's a way to clean up the streets and take care of ourselves."

"What do you mean?"

"Find a way that everyone wins. Cause what we've been doing ain't working," Max said, stubbing out his cigarette in the ashtray.

"Got that right. Let's talk about this more later. Gotta get our heads in the game."

Malone parked behind a black GMC van on the street. Malone and Max got out of the Chevy.

An odd-looking pair got out of the van. Leo was a clean-shaven, middle-aged white man with thick black glasses who would look at home working in IT. Johnny was a young black man that could easily be mistaken for a rookie despite having worked for the CPD for the past five years.

"Hey, guys. You good?" Malone said as he finished off his coffee.

"Yeah," Johnny said.

Leo nodded and opened the backdoors to the van. The four men gathered at the rear of the vehicle. Leo handed Malone a Mossberg 500 tactical shotgun. When Malone held the gun, it made him feel surprisingly comfortable. It was like a runner strapping on their shoes. The race was about to start. But this wasn't for fun. The stakes were life or death.

"Okay, we got a Latin King stash house here," Malone said. "Love to find Diego Garcia, a.k.a. Disciple Killer. He's been seen over here. Prick's been shooting up the South Side for a long time. Could be some other civilians in this two-flat, so we gotta get in and out. Have to assume these pricks are armed and high as a kite too."

Malone noticed the sweat beading on Johnny's forehead.

"I'll go in first," Malone said, "then Max and Leo." Malone pointed to Johnny. "You'll be covering our backs."

"Got it," Johnny said.

The transition from beat cop to the Gang Task Force would take some time. Malone figured Johnny needed a few more months on the job. Then he'd be alright. Until then, Malone would keep him under his wing.

Max turned to walk toward the building and froze in his tracks. "Damn. Smell that?"

"Shit, yeah. Probably a meth lab. Could be our location, or it could be upstairs. Let's go get the masks," Malone said.

"That shit smells like a skunk swimming in cat piss," Max said as the men walked back toward the van. "Remind me why I took this job again?"

"Because you can't sing or dance, asshole," Malone said with a chuckle as he got a gas mask from the back and pulled it down over his face.

The other men pulled on their masks too.

"Ready?" Malone's voice crackled through the speaker.

Everyone nodded in agreement.

"Okay, let's do this."

All four men rushed towards the two-story house. Malone led the way and stopped by the doorway before nodding to Max.

Max swung the battering ram and took out the door.

Malone barked out, "CPD! Freeze!"

A twenty-something white male in a stained white t-shirt

jerked his head up. "Shit!" He tipped over a glass container of a yellow liquid on the countertop and held a lighter on it.

Max watched the man run out the back door.

The fire spread and the smoke swallowed up the filthy kitchen.

Malone screamed, "Fire! Get back!"

He spun around and followed Max and the others back toward the door.

The fire spread around the table to the chairs, igniting the bottom floor. Malone scrambled out the door after Max and tried to catch his breath.

Someone screamed for help on the second floor.

Malone spotted an elderly woman at a window, banging on the glass with her bare fist.

"I just called it in—fire is a couple minutes out," Leo said.

"That's bullshit," Malone replied. "Get the ladder."

"It's not tall enough," Leo said.

Malone looked up to the second floor again.

"Don't fucking do it," Max barked. "Ain't nothing we can do until fire brings a truck with a ladder."

"Fuck that. Get our ladder. Meet me at the window," Malone said. He picked up the battering ram and ran back into the smoke. He had zero visibility and felt like a mouse in a maze. Finally, there was a break in the flames and he raced to the stairway. A quick swing of the battering ram and he was inside.

More noises. This time it was coughing.

Malone followed the sound and found the woman on the floor, unconscious. He leaned down to scoop her into his arms and peered out the window.

His men had pulled the van into the yard. A ten-foot ladder was held steady on the top of the vehicle by Johnny and Leo while the top of the ladder leaned against the house.

Max scaled up to the window where Malone could transfer the woman into his arms.

"You okay?"

Malone nodded once and passed the woman over.

He watched as Max then carried the woman down the ladder to Leo and Johnny. Once she was secure in their arms, Malone climbed down the latter to escape the flames licking at his heels.

"Thought you were fucking dead," Max said as he hopped down to the ground.

"Yeah," Malone said with a cough. "Me too."

"Why you gotta be the hero? You know how goddamn lucky you are?"

"Lucky? I feel like an ashtray," Malone said with a cough as he sat down on the van's bumper.

Max handed over Malone's flask. "Think you more than earned this."

Malone took a drink and slowly exhaled. Two fire trucks arrived along with an ambulance, pulling up to the curb next to them. Malone felt a weight off his shoulders as the EMTs loaded the woman onto a stretcher. Once she was secured, one of the EMTs turned his attention to Malone.

Malone tucked the flask into his pocket. "I'm fine. I'm fine," Malone said as he waved them off.

"You sure?"

"Yeah. Just need to catch my breath."

"You might wanna leave this asshole alone," Max said to the EMT. "Bastard just ran into a meth lab because he didn't wanna wait around for you."

"Shit—a meth lab? You know how lucky you are? Had to pull out five dead from a meth lab explosion yesterday."

"Yeah, yeah."

"Let me check your vitals?"

Malone ignored the question and turned toward Max.

"You see where the prick that bailed on us went?"

"No, I was getting the ladder for you. I'm sure he'll turn up. Probably at the hospital or something. We'll find him."

"Let's look around. He couldn't have gotten too far."

"You sure you're up for this? You look like shit."

Malone glared back at Max.

"Yeah, yeah. I know. Stupid question."

Malone took another drink.

"Hey boys, get your asses over here," Max said loudly toward Leo and Johnny.

"There's an APB on the runner," Leo said.

"Good," Malone said.

"Be nice if the prick is already in custody, you know?" Max shot back.

"Let's look around a little," Malone said as he walked over to his car. "We'll cover more ground if we split up."

The other men nodded and walked toward the van.

After driving up and down residential streets for half an hour, Max stretched his arms in the passenger's seat. "We ain't gonna find this prick on the street," he said.

"Probably right," Malone said, eyeing a gas station at the corner. "How 'bout some coffee?"

"Come on man, gas station coffee tastes like shit. Dunno how you drink that crap," Max replied.

"It ain't that bad."

Malone pulled into the gas station. As he got out of the driver's seat, he smirked when he saw Max getting out too. "Afraid you're gonna miss me?"

"No. I gotta take a piss."

"I guess that's allowed."

"If not, too fucking bad."

Malone went inside, walking over to the coffee machine, while Max hurried to the restroom.

As he poured a cup of coffee, Malone scanned the store.

He was alone other than the fifty-something man behind the counter.

Malone grabbed a granola bar off the counter and met Max at the register.

"Let me get that for you, since you're a hero and all."

"Thanks. I'm gonna hit the can too."

Malone entered the men's room and splashed some cold water on his face and dried off with a paper towel. Cleaning up helped him clear his head and get back into action. Then Malone met Max at the car.

"You ask the guy at the counter if he's seen our guy come in tonight?"

"Nope."

"Gimme a minute."

"You're kidding me, right? You think he's that dumb?"

"Just a minute."

Malone went back into the gas station. "Excuse me," he said.

The man behind the counter looked up from his book. "Yeah?"

Malone flashed his badge. "You see a white guy in a ratty white t-shirt, long black hair? Last hour or so? Probably acting really nervous and awkward."

"Matter of fact, I have. Bought a forty. Eyes wide as saucers and really nervous, just like you said."

"How long ago?"

"Ten, fifteen minutes. Somewhere round there."

"Okay, thanks."

Malone found a small alleyway behind the gas station. He drew his P226 and slipped past the dumpster. Then he saw a man with long black hair sitting on a plastic crate drinking a forty of malt liquor.

"Hey, asshole, you saving some for me?" Malone said as he pointed his gun at the meth cook.

"Shit man," he said, putting his hands up and dropping his bottle of malt liquor.

"You had a woman living right above your meth lab. Did you know that, or do you just not give a shit?"

No answer.

"I asked you a question, asshole. Did you know about the woman upstairs?"

"What the hell are you talkin' about?"

"That's what I thought. Stupid piece of shit."

Malone pistol-whipped the man in the head, knocking him to the ground.

"What the fuck you doing? I'm bleeding!"

The man sat up and had blood streaming down from his forehead dripping onto his dingy t-shirt.

"That's just a scratch."

"I'm bleeding man!"

Malone pistol-whipped him again, this time in the face.

He looked down at his P226 and saw blood on the barrel. He wiped it on the man's shirt.

"Get your lousy ass up." Malone holstered his gun, cuffed the man, and walked him around to the front of the gas station.

Max jumped out of the car. "Goddammit man, I ain't doubting you again."

"Mmm-hmm," Malone said with a smirk, "How 'bout you have someone take this little shit off my hands?"

"Gladly." Max took the perp and had him sit next to the car as he called it in.

Malone took a deep breath as he pulled a cigar out of the inside of his leather jacket and lit it. He watched Max pace in circles until he hung up and then he walked over to the driver's side window.

"Just called the others. Think this shitbird will talk?"

"Not sure, but it's always good to take a meth cook off the

street."

"Damn right. All in a day's work," Max said with a grin.

"You wanna go get a drink?"

"Raincheck. I got something planned with my old lady."

"This mean you got a new blow-up doll in the mail?"

"Very funny."

"If you ain't gonna go out, at least have a drink now."

"Absolutely."

Malone reached into his glove box and pulled out the flask. He took a slug of whiskey and passed it over to Max leaning on the side of the car. When Max handed back the flask, he put it in his pocket. Then, he saw Leo and Johnny pull up in the van behind them.

"Can you get a lift with them and process this guy? I'm beat."

"Yeah, you bet."

Max pulled the perp out of the car and walked him over to the van.

"Hey, Malone," Leo said. "Good work here. How'd you know?"

"Just a hunch."

"Great work."

"Thanks. See you tomorrow," Malone said as he climbed back into his car. He drove back to the crime scene and watched the fireman hosing down the smoking house. A month back he found a whole family dead inside from a meth lab explosion.

The sights. The smells. Another pull off his flask didn't erase the ghastly images in his mind. He thought of the woman from earlier today. If he hadn't gone into the building, she would have died too. He beat his hands on the steering wheel and let out a scream.

Today had renewed his passion for justice. Things had to change. Now.

CHAPTER TWO

Malone entered his small, one-bedroom apartment. The faded brown couch, outdated TV, and battered coffee table never offered much of a welcome. He scanned the contents inside his refrigerator: some condiments, a half-gallon of milk, leftover pasta, and a couple of bottles of Budweiser. While the pasta was in the microwave, he flipped through television channels until he found the Bears game.

When the microwave beeped, he stood up and yawned. After setting the food on the small, chipped brown coffee table, he took five steps back to the kitchen and grabbed a beer. He took a few bites of food and washed it down with a couple of swallows of Budweiser and pushed the food away. He laid down on the couch just as the Bears' quarterback threw an interception.

Malone groaned and closed his eyes. Just as he drifted off, his phone rang. He saw it was a local Chicago number.

"Yeah, hello?"

"Hello—Ryan? I'm Amy, a friend of your sister's. I'm with Sarah at Mercy Hospital. It's Andrew. He stopped breathing, and the doctors say he's overdosed on something."

Malone felt a weight drop in his stomach. He heard the words, but he didn't want to believe them. Not his family. Not this close to home.

"Shit, you gotta be fucking kidding. I'm on my way."

"We're in the ICU."

Malone turned on the siren and flew through all of the lights. He tried to ignore the countless negative thoughts flooding his mind.

The car fishtailed as Malone turned from Michigan Avenue onto 25th. Malone drove up to the hospital and slammed on the brakes, parking next to an ambulance. He ran to the ICU, and a nurse pointed him to the room.

Sarah was hunched over next to Andrew's bed. Andrew was hooked up to a respirator with tubes going up his nose. She clung to Andrew's hand and was quietly mouthing something as tears streamed down her face.

She flinched as Malone wrapped an arm around her. When she saw who it was, she sank against his chest.

"He seemed fine," Sarah said in a monotone voice. "Happy. He had a nice girlfriend. Last time we spoke he told me he was planning on going to DePaul next year. And—and now he's gotta be hooked up to a machine just to breathe."

Malone wasn't sure what to say. He kept his arm around Sarah and squeezed her shoulder. Malone's eyes stared off into the distance with a blank look on his face. He remembered the last time he was in this wing of Mercy Hospital. It was when James was born. He didn't want to look at his nephew surrounded by blinking lights and beeping sounds, alive only because of a machine that forced his lungs to work.

A doctor stepped into the room and cleared his throat. He had thin brown hair that turned grey at the temples, glasses, and a white coat. "I'm Dr. Walsh."

Malone let go of Sarah and stood up.

"The next few hours are critical. Andrew stopped

breathing for a while, and I'm afraid he's in a coma at the moment. We'll be monitoring him closely."

When the doctor left the room, Malone was right on his heels. "Dr. Walsh, can I talk to you?"

"Yes."

"I'm a police officer. This was an overdose?"

Dr. Walsh's face was grim as he said, "Yes, it was. Preliminary tests show it was a mixture of heroin and fentanyl. This is probably the fifteenth fentanyl overdose I've seen here in the last forty-eight hours."

"No fucking shit," Malone mumbled under his breath. "All of them heroin and fentanyl?"

"Yes. It's been on the rise for a while now, but this is the worst I've ever seen it."

"All of those overdoses here at Mercy?"

"Umm-hmm. Any other questions?"

"No, that's it. Thanks."

Malone went back into the hospital room and sat down next to Sarah. He continued to stare off in the distance, not looking at Andrew.

A few minutes later, Amy came into the hospital room, and Malone got up and gave her his seat. Malone fell into a light sleep on a waiting room chair using his leather jacket as a pillow. He woke up with a sore neck and looked up at the clock on the wall. An hour and a half had passed. He stuck his head into Andrew's room and said, "Want some coffee or something?"

Amy looked over and shook her head no.

Sarah was asleep in the chair near the bed. Her hand was still resting on Andrew's.

Malone took the elevator to the cafeteria. He saw a sign near the doorway stating the cafeteria was closed, but a few vending machines were nearby. Malone searched his pockets and put some coins into the coffee machine and watched the coffee stream down into the paper cup.

The local news was blaring on the television. "Chicago Police confiscated over five hundred thousand dollars worth of heroin in a routine stop last night," the news reporter said. Malone stood there listening as he let his coffee cool. A throbbing sensation started to well up in his gut and he could feel it coming to the surface. He pushed it back down and sipped his coffee.

The voice on the television said, "Up next, we've got an exclusive with Mayor Wallace. He'll be talking about the progress Chicago has made in the war on drugs."

Malone's mouth opened, but the words wouldn't come out. Anger erupted from deep inside and quickly turned to rage. He threw his cup of coffee at the television. Then he turned and punched the front of the vending machine. The glass shattered and shards flew across the floor. Before he knew it, a plastic chair was in his bloody hands. He launched the chair across the room.

Malone grabbed some napkins and wrapped his bloody knuckles. He stuffed his wounded hand into his jacket pocket as a hospital staff member came running into the room. He quickly climbed the stairs and walked back to Andrew's hospital room.

Dr. Walsh was inside standing next to Sarah and Amy. Their faces were ghostly pale and had no expression. Sarah looked up at Malone and opened her mouth to speak but couldn't.

Dr. Walsh stepped forward. "I'm sorry, but Andrew just went into cardiac arrest. We tried to resuscitate, but I'm afraid he didn't make it."

"Can't you put him on fucking life support?"

"I'm very sorry for your loss."

"This is bullshit!" Malone growled.

Malone stormed out of the room. When he got into his car, he took a drink from his flask but ran out of whiskey.

The phone only rang once before Max picked up.

"Come on, man. I'm about to get laid, you know?" Max said.

"I'm—uh—down at fucking Mercy. My nephew," Malone took a breath, finding the strength to bring the words up. "He overdosed on shit and didn't fucking make it."

"Motherfucker. I'm sorry man. That's some fucking shit. I'll be right there."

"Max?"

"Yeah?"

"Bring something to drink?"

"Yeah, will do."

Malone hung up and looked at his reflection in the rearview mirror and finally let out the scream he had been holding inside. The scream hurt Malone's ears but brought some relief at the same time. When he was able to calm down, he closed his eyes and let the whiskey do its job.

A few minutes later, Malone opened his eyes to the sound of Max tapping on the driver's window. He wound down the window.

"Got somethin' for ya buddy," Max said as handed over a bottle of Jameson's.

"Get your ass in here and join me for a taste."

Max walked over to the passenger's door and climbed in.

"How's Sarah?"

"She's a fuckin' mess."

"She's got a lot of shit going on, you know?"

"Mmm-hmm," Malone said as he took a swig.

"Gotta say your timing was something else. I was about to get laid."

"Sorry for the interruption, playboy."

"Don't worry about it. I jerked off in the car on the way

here. Hell, I might have done something special with that bottle," Max said.

Malone laughed and spit out some whiskey. "Asshole!"

"Yeah—how'd you know? Could you taste it?"

Malone and Max both laughed some more and kept drinking until they finished the bottle. Then it got quiet.

Malone tried to piece together what happened and none of it was making any sense. Andrew was a good kid. Not the kind of kid to ever do drugs. A numb feeling washed over him and it made him want to question everything.

Malone said, "Hey, you awake?"

"I—uh—I am now."

"Think I'm gonna go home. Get some sleep," Malone said.

"You okay to drive?"

"Hell yeah. I'm fine."

"You sure?"

"Yeah, I'm fine."

"Okay. You wanna drop me off at my car?"

"Where the hell'd you park?"

"I dunno."

Malone yawned.

"Fuck it then, I'm just gonna close my eyes for a minute."

"Works for me."

Malone woke up to the sound of a siren blaring as an ambulance pulled up to the hospital. Malone wasn't sure where he was at first and looked to his right and saw Max snoring in the passenger seat with a trail of vomit on the sleeve of his brown leather jacket. Malone chuckled to himself and, as he laughed, he realized how hungover he was. He leaned over, opening the glove box and startling Max.

"Whaa—? Huh?" Max jerked his head up and looked around.

"Hey man, we're here at Mercy. It's 4 AM now. You came over late last night. Just getting some aspirin out of the glove box."

"Oh—yeah. Yeah."

"You might need to hit the dry cleaners later."

"Huh?"

"You puked all over your fucking arm."

"Huh?" Max opened his eyes and glanced down at his sleeve. "Shit! Sonuvabitch!"

"It's okay man, I know a good dry cleaner."

"Goddamn it! Jenna gave me this jacket for Christmas last year. This is all your fault, you lush!"

"Yeah, yeah. Think there are some napkins in the glovebox."

Max found a stack of McDonald's napkins and started cleaning off his sleeve while cursing under his breath.

"Probably should go home and get cleaned up. We'll regroup in a few hours."

"Yeah, okay," Max said.

After a few minutes of driving around, Max found his car.

Malone went home and fell into his bed. A couple of hours later, he felt good enough to shower and put on a fresh change of clothes.

He started to piece together everything that happened. Andrew. Sarah. What the doctor said about fentanyl. The more Malone thought about it, the more he got pissed. He wasn't going to let this happen. Not in Chicago. Not in his town. Drugs were always hurting people, but nothing like this. Nothing on this scale. Someone had fucked up. Someone cut a batch with too much baking soda and the high wasn't good enough. The complaints came in and then someone else added the fentanyl to try to fix the batch.

Malone had been on the Gang Task Force for almost three years. Long enough to know how it worked. Long enough to make a few enemies and to know who the big players were. Malone loved the gig but knew it was only a matter of time until a new chief or captain would pull the plug or gut the team, making it useless. But that didn't matter. Today was today, and Malone was going to find whoever was responsible and make them pay.

He sat in the cold, black sedan watching the snowfall down, and took a sip of whiskey from his flask.

Max opened the door and got in. "Got your message. How the hell you still at it this morning?" Max said as he yawned.

"Guess I just hold my liquor better than you," Malone said, holding out the flask.

"That or you're just lit all the time," Max said with a chuckle and shook his head, declining the drink.

"Just having a taste to help with the hangover."

"Where we going?"

"Just want to see if anyone is out selling. Maybe we can get something outta somebody."

"Gotcha." Max took the flask from Malone and took a drink. Both men were quiet for a few minutes until Max broke the silence. "Been thinking about gettin' a tattoo."

"Oh yeah?"

"Yeah. Not sure what though."

"I don't want one, man. Not a big fan of needles."

"Pussy."

"Yeah, whatever. Maybe you should just get a nice heart with 'Mother' on it."

"Very funny."

"You mentioned something about finding a way for everyone to win. What'd you mean?"

"Say there was only one supplier for dope, and we had

designated zones for where selling happens. What the fuck would there be to fight about?" Max said.

"If they actually followed the rules, nothing. But they don't listen. They wanna just keep feuding and killing each other."

"Say they actually listened. And if they don't, we take their cash and their supply too."

"Like a penalty or something?" Malone said.

"Yeah, something like that."

"They'd buck against this. But if they actually followed the rules, it could work."

"Yep. I think it could."

"Something to think about."

"Sure is," Max said. He lit up a cigarette, cracked the window, and blew out the smoke. "You checked in with Sarah?"

"Not yet. She's got to be a mess."

"Yeah, I'm sure."

"Doc said Andrew overdosed on some fentanyl-laced heroin. Also said there's been a ton of them in the past couple days."

"Damn."

"Yeah, we gotta figure out what the fuck happened and then handle it."

"You know it."

The two men sat in silence for a few more minutes, waiting and watching.

Malone straightened his back and turned the ignition. "Alright, looks like no one is coming out this early. I know someone we can talk to indoors."

"Good. I'm freezing my balls off. When you gonna fix the heater?"

"Weren't you just calling me a pussy a few minutes ago? Maybe you need to toughen up yourself."

"Very funny."

Malone drove a few blocks and pulled up in front of a diner.

"Want me to come in too?" Max said.

"Let me go in first. Think my former CI might be working this morning. I'll be quick."

Max nodded and exhaled another puff of smoke.

Malone got out of the car and his back cracked as he stood up, bringing a small smile to his face. He walked into the diner lined with red booths, white countertops, and a black-and-white tile floor. He spotted a waitress in her early thirties with red hair pouring coffee for a customer at the counter. As he approached, he asked, "Wendy?"

She flinched and looked up with a big smile. "Malone. How are ya?"

"Good. Seen Mikey in here lately?"

"Yeah. He was in here yesterday."

"Any idea where he's staying these days?"

"Think he's staying at the shelter over by Ridgeland and 91st. It's a church."

"Okay, thanks. You look really good. I can tell you're staying clean."

"Yeah. If I'm not here, I'm either sleeping, at the gym, or in a meeting. Not saying it's easy. One day at a time."

"That's good. That's really good. You really look like you're doing great. I gotta go. Thanks again, Wendy."

Malone left a few bucks on the counter. When he got back to the car, he found Max sleeping. Malone bumped the horn.

"What the fuck?" Max lunged forward and his eyes sprung open. "Crazy asshole!" he screamed.

"Guilty as charged. Wake up. We gotta go over to the shelter on Ridgeland and 91st."

"Whatever. You're such a prick, know that? I should just beat your ass."

"Get in line, man. Get in line," Malone said.

The snow started to fall down harder and was sticking to the ground.

Malone could tell that Max was still groggy from the drinking and the brief nap.

It was a few short turns until they pulled up to the church. Malone parked and said, "You wanna go grab some coffee for us?"

"Yeah. Good idea."

He walked into the shelter and saw people crammed in the space. He assumed the weather had something to do with the large crowd. He also knew everyone in the room who was awake could tell that he was a cop. It was probably because of how Malone walked. He had that swagger, that been-there-done-that presence.

He scanned the room. Lots of kids with their mothers. Most were fast asleep on cots. He walked up and down the rows and found a dirty brown coat he recognized. Mikey was fast asleep in the corner on a cot, using his trench coat as a blanket. Mikey was rail-thin and in ragged clothes. His brown trench coat almost the same color as his skin tone.

He tapped Mikey on the shoulder and called his name. "Rise and shine, Mikey," Malone said. "It's your favorite person."

"Huh?" Mikey rubbed his eyes and slowly opened them. "Malone? Whatchu want?"

"I got a deal for you."

"Hell no, man. I ain't making no deals wit da five-oh."

"Just help me out. Then I'll help you out. That's it."

"I ain't no rat."

"Not saying you are. I just wanna know who is moving the most shit lately. Recent batch of shit was laced with fentanyl.

Over fifteen overdoses at Mercy in the past two days. That easily coulda been you, right?"

Mikey looked up at Malone. "Umm-hmm. Yeah, 'spose you're right."

"Just give me a name. Something I can use." Malone stared at Mikey, and it got quiet.

"I heard they moving some serious shit by the hotel on Canal Street. Right down from the convenience store."

"You mean by the Holiday Inn?"

"Yeah. Parking lot."

"What about your brother, Antoine?"

"He family. I ain't no snitch."

"Would your brother know any more?"

"Yeah, he'd know."

"Where is he?"

"No. No," Mikey shook his head repeatedly.

"You look like shit, Mikey. You're dope sick. I can help with that. Just give me a location."

"Shit man, I can't."

"Yeah, you can."

Mikey slowly moved his hands to his stomach as sweat beaded on his forehead.

"You know that ain't gonna get any better. It's only gonna get worse," Malone said.

"A'ight. A'ight. There's a strip joint over on Clinton. He's there a lot."

"Okay. Here you go," Malone pulled out a twenty and handed it to Mikey.

"Be careful. Buy from someone you trust."

"Yeah, a'ight, man." Mikey stuffed the cash in his sock and rolled over on the cot and closed his eyes.

Malone found Max waiting by the door with cups of coffee. He held out a cup and Malone took it.

"That warming you up at all?"

"Maybe a little. Gotta say I'd rather be drunk at home or asleep in my bed than freezing my balls off here."

"Tell me about it."

Malone took off his gloves and put them in his jacket pocket and moved his hands to the steering wheel. He stared out the windshield as he drove down the road.

"You gonna tell me what's up? You find out anything in there?"

"He says we need to check with Antoine Scott of the Gangster Disciples."

"Makes sense. He's high up on the food chain, and the Disciples move a lot of shit. You wanna rally the troops and visit Disciple territory today?"

"Yeah, but not right now. Let's do it later. I'm gonna catch some more sleep. Send a message to Johnny and Leo for me. We'll meet up at 10:00, usual place."

Max nodded and got out of the car in front of the station.

Malone rubbed his eyes and drank some more coffee. He drove down the road and pulled his foot off of the gas as he passed a brick two-story with a blue minivan in the driveway. Even after six months, he still found himself driving toward his old home. He moved his eyes back to the road and he pulled out his flask and took a drink.

A few minutes later, Malone parked on the street and walked toward a small apartment building. He went up the stairs to his second-floor apartment at the end of the hallway. Malone stepped inside and tumbled onto the couch. The sights and sounds of Andrew and Sarah at the hospital wouldn't go away. He got a bottle of whiskey from the cupboard and quickly drank some. When he closed his eyes, the images were still there, but now he couldn't make out faces. Like someone took away the glasses. The sound of the beeping machines stayed with him until it finally faded as he finally fell asleep.

A few hours later, Malone sat alone in the diner at a corner table. The image of Sarah crying over Andrew's lifeless body wouldn't go away. He sipped his black coffee and stabbed his eggs until the yoke broke and pooled on the white plate. He stared out the window, watching cars drive by until the rest of the GTF pulled into the parking lot in a dark blue SUV and walked into the diner.

Malone looked down at his watch and said, "Took your sweet ass time."

Max, Johnny, and Leo hung their heads.

Malone was a stickler for being on time. Always had been. He'd rather you show up hungover or even a little drunk than be a few minutes late.

Leo and Johnny both ordered a blueberry muffin and Max ordered pancakes, eggs, and bacon.

Once the waitress left, Malone started talking. "We need to find the leader of Gangster Disciples, Antoine Scott. If we can't get him, then we need one of his soldiers to roll on him."

"Good luck with that," Max said.

"Do we have an address on him?" Johnny asked, taking a bite of his muffin.

"Nothing reliable. But when something happens, Antoine is either involved or knows about it. Maybe he's the asshole who put the shit on the streets. If not, he probably knows who did it."

Malone took another sip of his black coffee and followed with a forkful of eggs.

"Good news is we know he's often at a strip joint over on South Clinton Street," Malone said. "I think it's Déjà Vu or Pink Monkey or something. It's a start."

"That's the Purple Monkey. Just a word of warning—you

might get the clap or some other VD just by walking into the place," said Max.

"You'd know," Malone said with a chuckle.

"Screw you," Max shot back.

"Leo, we gotta get an address on this guy—in case this strip joint is a bust."

"I'll do some digging," Leo said as he ate the last bite of his muffin.

"Johnny, help Leo out. There's gotta be a paper trail on this prick somewhere."

"Yeah," Johnny agreed. "Will do."

Leo and Johnny left the diner.

Malone finished his coffee. "Okay. Let's get our asses down to the station."

"Hold on, my food ain't come out yet. I'm starving," Max said.

"Show up on time and you ain't got that problem," Malone said.

"Asshole."

"That's Sargent Asshole to you, shithead," Malone said as he got up and tossed some cash on the table.

"Come on," Max said, "It's gonna be ready any second now."

Malone walked toward the door and Max saw the waitress come out with a plateful of food in her hand. "Dammit, Malone. Let me at least have 'em box it up."

Malone started the car and revved the engine.

"Motherfucker," Max muttered under his breath as he heard the revving. "Can you please box that up for me?"

"Sure, hun. Just be a minute," the waitress said as she took the plate and walked back to the kitchen.

Max ran out to Malone's car. "They're boxing it up. Gimme a minute."

Malone smiled and said, "Yeah, okay. No problem."

"Asshole," Max said as he went back inside the diner.

Thirty seconds later Max climbed into the car with a white Styrofoam container and pulled out a piece of bacon.

"You gonna share some?"

"Don't make me draw my piece out on you," Max said with a mouthful of bacon.

Malone smiled. "You'd do it, wouldn't you."

"Hell yeah, I would. I'm fucking starving. Don't mess with a man's food," Max said, tossing some pancake into his mouth.

"I'm just fucking around with you."

"I know. What's your history with this guy?"

"Had a few run-ins with Antoine about three years ago. You were still with Vice. Arrested him twice. He was just an up and comer, head of the bangers on the corners that were moving a lot of shit. He ain't no fan of mine, but he doesn't hate me either. I've always been straight with him."

"How's it gonna go over, seeing you in the strip joint?"

"Probably won't do a damn thing 'cause he'll have a crew with him and know I don't got shit on him. Figure, four maybe five guys with him, all packing."

"Good to know."

"Uh-huh. Can't pull any cowboy shit in there with this prick."

The two men walked into the police station lobby, went up the stairs, and headed down the hall toward the GTF office. It was nothing more than a small, outdated conference room with four walls, four desks, four computers, a whiteboard, and a couple of grey filing cabinets against the wall.

Leo and Johnny were both at their desks staring at their computer screens.

"Find anything?"

"In twenty minutes?" Leo said.

"Yeah. I know you're good."

"Oh yeah, already found him and have him in custody."

"Now that's what I like to hear."

"We've been working on finding his mom's address." Leo motioned toward a piece of paper on his desk and Malone picked it up.

"That's good. Gotta visit your mom, right."

"Yeah, at some point you do."

"Keep digging."

"Will do," Leo said as his eyes flicked back down to the computer screen.

"Max, you got any contacts at that strip joint?" Malone asked.

"Yeah, I know a girl named Vi there who normally works nights."

"Think she'd do a favor for you?"

"Depends on the favor."

"If Antoine shows up, we need her to take him to the back for a private dance."

"I think she'll be up for that."

"Good. We just need him alone."

Max nodded.

"You got another plan if Vi ain't working or won't do it?" Max said.

"I'm working on it," Malone replied.

"We'll let you know what we find at his mother's house," Leo said.

Malone and Max walked out of the station together. Max was wearing a big cheesy grin.

"Why are you smiling like that?" Malone said.

"Man, you just got me out of doing paperwork, and now we're hitting a strip joint. I kinda like having you in charge," Max joked.

"Come on, now. I'm full of surprises."

CHAPTER THREE

Malone pulled his car into the parking lot behind the Purple Monkey. Despite the name, the place didn't look like a strip joint. The building was constructed of newer orange-colored bricks and resembled a warehouse. It was surrounded by other brick buildings, making it easy to miss.

"Think that's Vi's yellow car over there," Max said.

"How the hell you know that?"

Max smiled and said, "You know, if she agrees to this she's gonna want some cash for the favor."

"Yeah, I figured. That's no problem."

Max reached for the door handle, then hesitated.

"Why didn't you say something last night?"

"Huh?"

"About the strip joint."

"Wanted to tell the whole team at the same time."

"Yeah. What if we missed our shot by fucking around this morning talking to everyone? Could be a helluva lot further than we are now."

"I ain't no fucking psychic, you know? Just go see if she's working and make it quick. No lap dances, got it?"

"I can't help it. The ladies all love me." Max flashed a smile revealing all of his teeth and got out of the car. Malone pulled out his flask and took a drink as he watched Max enter the building. He listened to some music on the radio until the ads came on and changed the channel to sports talk radio.

Malone's mind flooded with all of the possible scenarios that could take place meeting with Antoine. Squeeze too hard and he'd have a serious enemy. Go too light and the Gangster Disciples would start to think they could outmuscle the GTF. As a radio caller ranted about the Bears, Malone took another pull. He yawned and closed his eyes, falling into a light sleep.

A few minutes later, he woke up as Max opened the car door.

"Vi was there. We're good to go. Just gotta point 'em out to her and throw some cash her way."

"That's fine. She say how much?"

"No, but gotta figure at least a couple hundred."

"Okay. We'll come back tonight around seven."

"Hey, man. Gimme a taste. Think I can't smell that? It's like a goddamn bar in here."

"Yeah, yeah. Here you go," Malone laughed as he pulled the flask out of his jacket and handed it over.

"You gotta get some mints or something. This shit stays with you more than you think."

"Uh-hmm."

After hitting a convenience store for a pack of mints, they went back to the station. Malone walked into the GTF office with an unlit cigar in his mouth.

"That a victory cigar? You already solved the case?" Leo said.

"Not yet. Almost there though," Malone said with a sly smile as he sat down in his chair. He put the cigar into a black, leather cigar holder and left it on his desk.

"Find out anything?" Malone asked Johnny and Leo.

"Not much yet. Any idea how many people in Chicago with the last name Scott?" Leo said.

"I'm betting a few," Malone said.

"Over two hundred on the South Side alone," Leo said.

"No shit," Max replied.

"And most of these records aren't current," Johnny said. "So we're spending most of our time verifying everything."

"We're gonna head back to the strip joint at about seven tonight," Malone said. "I want you both there as backup. We'll likely have a circus on our hands with a bunch of fuckups packing a lot of heat. Never know what could happen."

The other men nodded.

"Johnny, looks like you get to go on your first stakeout," Max said. "And best of all, I'm gonna be drinking and getting a lap dance while you're in the car wearing a fucking diaper."

"What?"

Malone smiled. "He ain't kidding. We dunno how long it's gonna be, so until you train your bladder, you better not drink anything or you're wearing a diaper."

"You're kidding."

"Tell him, Max."

"He don't wanna hear about that."

"You fucking tell him, or I will."

"It was my first stakeout with this bastard here," Max threw a wadded-up piece of paper toward Malone. "We were waiting at the fence for some stolen TVs. I didn't believe him, and I ended up having an accident as we got out of the car arresting the bastards with the shipment."

"What the hell happened?" Johnny said.

"Hold on. I'm getting there. I had to piss really bad. And I found an empty pop bottle. Then the shipment of TVs came in while I was going. I'll let him fill you in on the rest."

"There was a damn trail of piss that started inside the car and led all over the crime scene," Malone said, laughing.

"No shit," Johnny said.

"No, it was piss," Malone said with another laugh.

"Hey, once this horse gets out of the stable, takes time to put him back," Max said. "Know what I'm saying?"

"Whatever you say, Mr. Ed," Malone smirked as he glanced down at his watch. "It's almost 5:30 now, why don't we get a bite and then roll out?"

"You hungry after that story?" Johnny said.

"That shit don't bother me. How 'bout some Giordano's?" Max said.

"Works for me," Leo said.

After dinner, Malone sat alone in his car parked near the Purple Monkey. He could see Johnny and Leo on the other side of the parking lot inside of a dark SUV. Malone yawned and started to think maybe pizza before a stakeout wasn't the best idea. He felt like he had a brick in his stomach and now he just wanted a nap. Malone hated stakeouts anyway. It usually meant a lot of waiting around in an uncomfortable car and very little action.

The worst part was nine times out of ten, the perp would go down in a matter of seconds. No fight required, just a simple takedown. It's nothing like the movies or TV. Nothing quite like being stuck watching doors or windows for hours on end, eating shitty food and waiting for something to happen. Malone looked at his watch. 7:50. Max went inside around 7:05. No contact since.

Malone figured Max was getting his third lap dance by now and was well on his way to getting shit-faced. Maybe that was the good thing about having pizza. It would take Max longer to get drunk.

As he sat there, Malone had a bad feeling in his gut. He wanted to be wrong, but the longer he waited, the worse it got. Malone planned on waiting another five minutes before going inside. He rubbed his eyes with his palms, then raked his fingers through his hair. He took a drink from the flask, hoping it would help his nerves. Malone's phone rang, and the name Ann flashed on the screen. He let the phone ring again before deciding to answer.

"Hello," Malone said, partially coughing after the word came out of his mouth.

"Are you okay?"

"Hi. Yeah. I'm fine. How are you?"

"James has a basketball game on Saturday. Can you take him?"

"I think so, but lemme check and get back with you."

"He hasn't seen you in weeks and keeps asking about you. Why don't you take him?"

"I will if can. Look—I gotta run."

"Wait, I need some money. James needs new shoes and pants and don't forget the zoo..."

"I'll send you some. Look, I gotta go."

Malone hung up and took another drink. Every fucking time she called she wanted more money. He put the lid on the flask as his phone rang again.

"He's here. Right rear corner," Max said.

"How many with him?"

"Six total."

"Shit. You point him out to the girl?"

"Yep, just did."

"Be right there."

Malone stretched his arms out to the side as he stepped quickly through the door. A mix of pink and purple lights flashed on the walls cutting through the shadows. The bright spotlights focused on a blonde dancer on stage. There were mirrors on the walls and the ceiling.

Malone spotted Antoine sitting in the corner with five other men. He saw PeeWee, muscle for the Disciples, but didn't recognize the others. Malone walked over to the bar and ordered a beer. He paid the bartender and saw Max midway across the room near the stage. Malone turned his barstool and sat with his back toward Antoine and watched him in the mirror. He nursed his beer as a dancer approached Antoine's table. Malone looked over at Max who slightly nodded once, confirming that was the right girl. Vi had brown hair and was wearing a white bikini with a fluffy pink boa draped over her shoulders.

Within a few minutes, she had the boa around Antoine's neck and leaned over whispering in his ear.

Antoine got up from the horseshoe-shaped seat and escorted Vi toward the private rooms in the back. They slipped past a velvet rope and went in the third door on the left. Malone left his beer at the bar and walked toward the private rooms. Just outside the door, he hung back, waiting for Max. Once Max got close, Malone said, "I'm gonna go chat with Antoine. Keep an eye out for Peewee over there. He's a real head case. Don't want a fucking shootout. Call backup if you need 'em."

"Got it."

Vi was giving Antoine a lap dance in the middle of the room when he entered.

"Sorry to interrupt, but we gotta talk. It'll just take a minute," Malone said, holding up his badge.

"What the fuck man?"

Vi got up and left the room.

Malone stood in front of Antoine and said, "Calm down or I'll take your ass downtown for that piece you've got in your pants. We both know that'll break probation. Put that shit on the floor—slowly."

Antoine stared at Malone and his lip tightened into a scowl, but he slowly put his Magnum on the tile floor.

"A nigga can't get a break," Antoine said.

"Cry me a river."

Malone leaned forward and picked up the Magnum. The safety was on. The serial number scratched off. He laid the gun flat in his hands with the handle in his right hand and the barrel in his left.

"Got anything you wanna tell me about?"

"Nope. Nothin' I can think of."

"Sure about that?"

Antoine didn't say a word.

"Fine, play it that way," Malone sneered. "Some bad shit came in over the past week, laced with fentanyl. And there's been a shit-ton of ODs all over. What do you know about it?"

"Huh? I dunno shit."

"Look, I know you're gonna sell drugs. You're gonna have your little wars with other gangs. That's what gangs do. Just tell me what fucking happened." Malone opened the gun's cylinder and the shells toppled into his hand. He examined them and stuffed them in his jacket pocket.

"I dunno shit. Wasn't us. Not our thing."

"I'm not saying this was you," Malone said, pointing the empty Magnum at the ground. "Maybe a member of the cartel did it. Maybe one of your crew fucked up and got greedy. Someone did that and you might not know shit. But this mess left a bunch of bodies. Young as fifteen years old. That's a fucking kid. Good idea to start talking."

"I don't fucking know."

"There ain't a goddamn thing happens on the South Side without you knowing about it."

"Shit man. You talking to Mikey, huh?"

Malone smiled. "Someone's gotta look out for him."

"A'ight. Fine. Why'd we do that shit? That's bad business. I ain't biting the hand that feeds, ya know?"

"Then who did it?"

"Probably the Kings."

"Why would they do it?"

"Crank up the heat on us while they do their thing. Got you in my face, right?"

"Power grab by the Latin Kings, huh?"

"Yeah, they be stirrin' up shit and takin' out niggas too. You come in an' bang on us, while they settin' up shop on new corners."

Malone leveled his eyes.

Antoine stared right back.

"We done motherfucker? Dat's all I know. Send the bitch back in."

"Yeah, okay." Malone set the Magnum on the ground and walked out of the room as Vi came back inside.

"How'd it go?" Max said as he met Malone by the door.

"He thinks the Latin Kings did it. That or a cartel fuckup."

"You believe him?"

"He's a piece of shit drug dealer and gang leader," Malone said and then coughed to clear his throat. "But you ever heard of a dealer killing their own customers when they can make money off them?"

"Good point."

"Let's get the hell outta here—smells too much like vomit and VDs in this joint."

"Ya know, you kinda get used to it," Max said with a smile.

"Let's go to a classier joint."

"Only if you're buying."

"Cheap ass bastard."

CHAPTER FOUR

Malone and Max went into Dugan's Irish Pub, sat down at the bar, and ordered their drinks.

"Ain't too busy," Max pointed out.

"Bulls are playing tonight. Tickets are probably pretty cheap."

"You got anything riding?"

"Nope. Lost enough last month."

"Hear that," Max agreed.

The front door chimed as Leo and Johnny walked inside.

"Looks like the cavalry's here."

"Find out anything?" Leo asked.

"Yeah, he wasn't too fond of cops. Especially cops stopping a lap dance."

"Shocking," Leo said. "Any other great insights?"

"I'll tell you more in a minute. Let's grab the table in the back. Whaddya want?"

"Doesn't matter to us as long as you're buying," Leo said, flashing a quick smile at Malone.

"Damn, you sound like Max." Malone turned to Max. "See what a bad influence you are on everyone?"

"Who, me?" Max joked with a wide smile.

The group moved to a more private table on the other side of the bar. They were quiet as a waiter placed a tray of shots on the table. Malone was the first to raise his glass. "Here's to having less assholes on the street."

"Hold up—you're taking an early retirement?" Max said.

All four laughed and threw back their shots.

"Don't you wish. Think you've had enough to drink tonight, dickhead."

"Don't think so," Max said. "Room ain't spinning or nothing."

"What'd you find out from Antoine?" Leo asked.

"He thinks the Latin Kings or whoever supplied their shit did it."

"Could be covering his sorry ass," Max said.

"Yeah, maybe. But why would they take out their own customers?"

"Who says Antoine or any dealer cares? They got an endless supply of junkies waiting in the wings," Max said.

"Say Antoine's right," Leo suggested. "That means the Kings are smart. Probably doing it to find some new real estate."

"Yep," Malone agreed as he took another shot.

"What if it's just flat out easier and cheaper to make it using Fentanyl?" Leo said, then grabbed his shot. "I know you're not gonna like this, but maybe you need to call the DEA."

"Those assholes don't know shit," Malone said.

"I know you're not a fan. But a phone call couldn't hurt, right?"

"Yeah, you're right. I'll do it tomorrow if you promise to stop talking about those pricks," Malone said with a laugh.

"At least we'll know," Leo said. "I'll buy you another round if it keeps you from being pissed at me."

"Deal. But make it quick."

Leo ordered another round of shots.

"How many suppliers are bringing shit into town?" Max asked.

"About four or five cartels," Leo said. "Sinaloa is the largest. You've got the Jalisco New Generation Cartel. The New Gens are a spinoff of the Sinaloa. Then Knights Templar. Los Zetas. Each is sending shipments here all the time. And they're using different mules too."

"And we're busy dealing with gang wars and corner boy shit," Malone commented.

"Yeah, for sure. Until we have access to the supply chain, we can't stop it. It's just too many vehicles."

"So we gotta rattle some cages until something pops up," Max said.

Malone threw back another shot. "Exactly. Leo, Max—look at the Latin Kings. Talk to Narcotics too and see if they have anything. I'm gonna see what else I can find out with my CIs, and tomorrow I'll check in with the Feds."

"What about me?" Johnny asked.

"Back up Leo and Max. Whatever they need, you help them. Got it?"

Johnny nodded.

"Okay. Enough talking shop," Max said. "You're killing my buzz."

"Sorry to interrupt you, player. Figured you were out there getting blown in the alley an hour ago."

Max smiled back at Malone.

"Yeah, she liked it so much she paid me. You could say that drink in your hand is courtesy of Mr. Happy."

Malone spat out some of his drink with a laugh. "Shit—no more for you," he said. "You're losing it."

"Whatever you say, boss."

"Good answer. Hell, I guess one more round wouldn't

hurt." Malone signaled the waiter. After drinking for another half hour, they called it a night.

———————

Malone drove past his apartment down Canal Street until he came to a small townhouse. Sarah's car was parked nearby. He rapped his knuckles against the door and waited. No answer. He lit a cigar from his pocket, leaning against the doorframe. After another slow draw on his cigar, he knocked again. Still no answer.

"Shit," he mumbled aloud as he walked around to the backdoor. It was unlocked, so he helped himself inside.

He spotted a stack of documents on the kitchen table and flipped through it using the porch light streaming in through the window. Credit card statements, some junk mail. The credit card statement on the top was for $9,588.77. Another below was for $6,982.56.

"Fucking shit," he said under his breath. "And that's before the hospital bill." He sighed out loud and slowly set them down on the table.

"Sarah?"

There was no response.

He moved into the living room and found her asleep on the couch with a bottle of vodka nearby, her face covered in a soft blue tint from the glowing TV on the other side of the room—an infomercial for a juicer. Leaning in close, Malone could hear her breathing deeply. He placed a small trash can on the floor near Sarah's head. Then he draped a red blanket over her. He sat down in the recliner and drank what was left of the vodka as images of vegetables being crammed into a juicer flashed on the TV screen. Soon, he fell asleep in the recliner.

A few hours later, Malone was jolted awake by the sound

of Sarah vomiting in the trash can. He waited until she finished before saying anything.

"Sarah," he whispered. "Sarah—it's Ryan."

She jerked back as she woke up and stared at him with wide eyes.

"It's okay," he reassured her. "I just wanted to come and check on you. Go back to sleep. If you need anything, I'm here."

"Okay," Sarah whispered before passing out again.

Malone couldn't get comfortable sleeping in the recliner and wasn't even sure he had actually slept. A couple of hours later, he decided to get up while it was still dark outside. He stretched his arms above his head, and his back cracked. The empty bottle of vodka and the trash on the floor bothered him, so he threw them away. Then he made coffee, took some aspirin, and sat back down in the recliner, and watched a rerun of Happy Days.

About an hour later, Sarah woke up.

"Hey," he said. "It's me. You doing okay?"

"Wha-? I—uh—my head's killing me," Sarah whispered.

"Here's some aspirin," Malone said, handing her the small white bottle.

"Thanks," Sarah said as she swallowed the pills.

"You okay?"

Tears swelled in her eyes.

"I know I'm drinking too much. But drinking is the only thing that helps. It's the only way I can sleep."

"Yeah. You're gonna feel better soon. I know it." Malone wasn't able to say anything else. He then got up and said, "I better go in. I'll—uh—check on you soon, okay?"

"Just stay awhile with me, okay?"

"Yeah." Malone sat down on the couch next to Sarah until she fell back asleep.

CHAPTER FIVE

Malone noticed his phone ringing as he walked outside to his car.

"Where the hell are you?" Max said.

"Hey. At Sarah's."

"How's she doing?"

"Like you'd expect."

"Sorry to hear that. Are you coming in? Could really use your help."

"I'll be there in about an hour."

"Okay, good. We're swimming in paperwork here looking for leads."

"How fun."

"Not so much. Misery loves company."

"I gotta do something first, then I'll be in."

After a quick shower and change of clothes at home, Malone hit the streets. He finished his cigar standing outside of a pizza shop two doors down from Windy City Pawn. Most of the inventory was clean, but Malone knew there were always a few dirty items in the backroom. The store was too close to both Latin King and Gangster Disciple territory to be completely legit.

The pawn shop had guitars on the wall, rows of washers and other household appliances, bicycles in the aisle, stereos on shelves, and televisions lined up behind the counter. A glass case was filled with an assortment of watches, necklaces, earrings, rings, knives, and cell phones. An older black man with grey-tinted hair stood behind the counter.

"Hey Erv," Malone said.

"Malone. Ain't seen you in a while."

"You good?"

"Yeah. How are you?"

"Be good when this hangover lets up."

"You Irish man. Should be 'usta that by now, right? Whatcha lookin for?"

"You know what I like. Got anything new?"

"Yeah, I think I got somethin' you'll like." Erv pointed to a silver diver watch in the corner of the glass case. "Really nice, ain't it? Got a good deal for ya here."

Malone glanced at the jewelry and his eyes bounced back directly at Erv.

"That ain't too bad. Maybe next time. I need to talk shop for a second. What have you heard about the Kings or the Disciples?"

"Malone—look man—I ain't stirrin' up no shit. I say something, it points to me, dey'll burn dis place to the ground and probably kill me too. You know I'm right. Why you be askin' me questions like that?"

"I gotta know. Bad batch took my nephew a couple days ago."

"Shit. I'm sorry man."

Another customer entered the store, jingling the bells on the door.

"Tell you what, take a look over here," Erv said. "I got

something that's perfect for ya here." He pulled out some diamond earrings.

"Nice."

"Your girl would love these," Erv said.

"I dunno, let me think about it."

"Sure, no problem. Let me give you my card. I'll jot down the details for you too."

Erv wrote something on the card with a pencil and gave it to Malone.

"Thanks."

"Yep. You have a good one now."

Malone walked out of the store and flipped over the card. It read: *Ramon's sick. New Corona coming.* Malone stared at the information in his hand and put it into his back pocket. If this was true, this might of been a factor in his making parole. It also meant the Latin Kings would be changing things up a bit. They would likely be out earning more and doing more damage than usual trying to impress their new leader. It fit with what Antoine said.

The wind picked up, making Malone stuff his hands into his jacket. He took a deep breath and pulled out his phone and waited for the call to go through. "Yeah, this is Special Agent Green."

"Hi Alex. Ryan Malone."

"Ryan, I've been waiting for your assessment from the third quarter."

"Yeah, I'll have it soon. Got a quick question for ya."

"I need that assessment as soon as possible."

"Yeah, I'll take care of it. Seeing a big surge in Fentanyl-laced heroin here in Chicago. What's it looking like on your end?"

"Fentanyl production has been increasing all across the country. It's cost-effective because it's made in laboratories, not grown in the wild. It's approximately fifty times stronger than heroin. The cartels find it more profitable, too."

"How much more profitable we talking?"

"About five to six times more. Fentanyl can be snorted, injected, or mixed with heroin. Of course, it's also available in pill and patch forms."

"Fuck me," Malone mumbled to himself.

"Most of the Fentanyl is being imported from Mexico and then going to the west coast, often California."

"Do we know the sources in Mexico?"

"Currently, the Sinaloa Cartel and Juarez Cartel are the two primary sources. Didn't you read the update I sent you last month?"

Malone didn't answer.

"Tell me—when will you have the third-quarter assessment ready for me?"

"By Friday."

"Okay, remember I'll need all of your documentation included as an attachment."

"Yeah—yeah. Sure thing. Will do."

Malone hung up and took a pull from his flask and drove back to headquarters.

CHAPTER SIX

Malone walked into the GTF office and saw each team member at their desk surrounded by manilla file folders and fast-food wrappers.

"Wow, looks like you're having a real party here," he said.

Max waved a middle finger at Malone.

"Oh yeah," Johnny said, "Lunch and sorting through files."

"Got some new info," Malone said as he sat down at his desk. "Word on the street is that Ramon's sick and the Latin Kings are going to have a new Corona. Assuming this is right, might be a factor in how he got parole. The bangers will want to impress the new boss. I talked to the Feds too. The cartels make a shit-ton more profit using Fentanyl. Shit's lethal as hell. You can snort it, shoot it, take it as pills, even mix it with other shit. This shit's even used to tranquilize goddamn elephants."

"No shit," Johnny said. "What the hell are we gonna do?"

"Same thing we always do—go after the bad guys. Get as much of this shit off the street as we can," Max said.

"Damn straight. Still the same goal, finding whoever's

responsible. Nothing's really changed. We're still playing chess here. Gotta keep clearing off the board, one fucking piece at a time."

Max sipped his coffee and pulled out a picture from a manilla folder.

"I got something too," Max said as he held up a black and white picture of a Hispanic man in his late twenties with a shaved head and beard. "Know our friend Diego Garcia—Disciple Killer—who skated on us the other day?"

"Tell me you got something on that piece of shit," Malone said.

"Yeah, DK ain't in the wind no more."

"No shit. Whaddya got?"

"My CI says her friend placed DK in Little Village. She's heading over there right now and will confirm."

"See?" Malone said to Johnny. "This kinda shit's why a cop's only as good as his informants."

Johnny nodded. "Yeah, for sure."

Leo pulled up DK's file on his computer. "Looks like DK has another outstanding arrest warrant," he said.

"Yeah, no surprises there," Malone said.

"What's the play?" Johnny asked.

"Gear up. We're gonna go round up this prick. We'll roll out in thirty minutes."

Malone would normally roll in on a perp nice and early. Catch him while he's still groggy or snoring in bed. In and out before sunrise. But with someone as dangerous as DK he wanted to get visual confirmation before storming in. Malone parked the car and looked over at Max in the passenger seat. Johnny was in the van behind Leo.

"We're good to go once we get confirmation from the CI," Malone said into his two-way. "Shouldn't take too long." Max pulled his phone out of his pocket and typed a text message.

"Gotta admit," Max said as he puffed on a cigarette, "I ain't in no hurry to go out in the fucking cold. Not that it's much better in here."

"Quit complaining, man," Malone said as he lit his cigar. "I think heat's starting to work."

"If you say so," Max said as he blew a puff of smoke. Thirty seconds later, Max received a message. "Yeah, she said he's here. She's downstairs."

"Okay, we just received confirmation," Malone said into his two-way. "Let's do this." He got out of the car, pulled a shotgun from the trunk, and adjusted his body armor. He looked over at Max who already had his vest on. Johnny walked up to the car holding a battering ram.

"Won't need that," Max said to Johnny. "She's smart. Door'll be open."

Johnny nodded and put the battering ram back in the van and came back to the car.

"You guys know the drill—assume DK and a few of his homeboys are in there ready to take out as many cops as possible. Play it smart. Cover each other's ass. Got it?" Malone said.

Max, Leo, and Johnny all nodded.

"Okay, good. Let's go."

The men quickly ran to the front door. Malone reached out to turn the doorknob and it was unlocked. He slowly opened the door and saw a woman sitting on the couch in a pink shirt. She had a hand in the air, pointing up while mouthing the word "upstairs." Malone nodded and quickly pointed at Max and then to his CI.

"Come here," Max whispered, taking her hand. He took her outside and gave her some cash for a cab and quickly came back inside. Max nodded to Malone and, together, they continued moving through the living room. The room was covered in empty pizza boxes, an assortment of bottles, junk food wrappers, and burnt spoons. On the opposite side of the living room, he spotted a stairwell that led to a hallway splitting left and right.

When the men reached the top, Malone directed Johnny and Leo to go to the left and motioned for Max to go to the right with him.

Malone got to the bedroom door and saw a shirtless black man move in the bed. "Chicago Police," he yelled. "Freeze!"

The man in the bed immediately raised his hands and the blanket fell down, revealing that he was naked.

"I didn't do nuthin," the man said with a muffled voice.

"Shut up. Keep your hands up and don't fucking move," Max said.

The man looked back with wide eyes as gunshots rang out from the other side of the house.

The naked man jumped when he heard the gunshots.

"Freeze, asshole! Don't move," Malone said as he aimed the shotgun at the man. "Hands behind your head. Put your face down on the bed."

The man listened.

"You got this?" Malone said to Max.

Max nodded his head.

Malone hurried down the hall and stopped at the doorway and saw Leo and Johnny inside.

"What the hell happened?" Malone said.

"Perp wouldn't put his gun down," Leo said. "Took two rounds to the chest to get him to drop his piece."

"DK?"

"Yeah," Johnny replied and followed Malone to the other bedroom.

"Okay. Let's book needle dick, and get outta here," Malone said as he entered the other bedroom.

Max nodded slightly and looked at the naked man. "Get the hell up—slowly, and keep your hands on your head." The man slowly rose up and Leo stepped forward and cuffed him. "On your feet asshole," Max said, keeping the gun steady on him.

"I'm gonna call this in," Johnny said.

"Hold off for a minute. Go find some clothes or blanket or something for this prick," Malone said. "Might even have something in the van."

Johnny nodded and left the room. Malone went into the other bedroom and saw the blood-covered body spread out on the bed. Probably about 25 years old. He noticed a large tattoo on the man's chest. It was a cross with the words sólo Dios puede juzgarme—"Only God can judge me"— scrolled on it. Malone took a deep breath. Another bad guy off the street. He went back to the other bedroom and saw Max with his Glock pointing at the man in the bed.

"Where the hell is the stash, shithead?" Max said.

"Huh?" the man said as he started to nod off.

"You know what the fuck I'm talking about. Where's the shit? Tell me."

Malone stood in the doorway with his arms crossed as Max punched the man in the head, sending his head into the wall.

"Better start talking, junkie," Max ordered. "The more you make us look, the more trouble you're in."

Max went to punch him again but Malone stepped forward. "Okay, that's enough," he said. "This ain't working. He's higher than a fucking kite. Go check under the sink, the toilet, the vents."

Once everyone left the room, Malone pulled out his P226 and aimed it at the man's head.

"Better start talking. Where's the shit?"

"Huh?"

Malone held the gun closer and pressed the barrel on the man's head. "Don't tell me you don't know," he said. "Where the fuck is it?"

"Uh—it's under the sink," the man mumbled.

Malone holstered his gun. "Under the sink!" he yelled.

Leo hurried into the bathroom. "Yeah, got something here," he said. "Looks like about four kilos of heroin and some pretty serious cash."

"Bring it out here."

Leo walked into the bedroom with a black bag in his hands.

Malone looked back at the man on the bed who had passed out. "That all of it?"

"Looks like he ain't gonna be saying much more for a while," Max said.

"Go get a trash bag to put the dope in," Malone said to Leo.

"Here's our shot, man," Max said. "You ready to get a taste?"

Malone nodded his head. "Guess we gotta start sometime."

Leo came back with the trash bag and handed it to Malone. "See if Johnny found anything for this guy to wear. And call this in."

"Yeah, sure," Leo said as he stepped back into the hallway.

Malone pulled the dope out of the black duffel bag, piled it all in the trash bag, and picked it up.

"About goddamn time to get a raise," Max said.

Malone laughed. "You sure about this?"

"What the hell do you think?" Max smiled and took the bag from Malone's hands.

Malone looked out the window as Max opened the trunk and placed the black duffel bag inside. Malone turned back to the cuffed man on the bed who was out cold and shook his head in disgust.

"Couldn't find anything for him to wear," Johnny said as he looked down and saw the trash bag full of dope.

"Don't matter, he's out cold now. He's breathing fine though. We'll let EMS take care of him."

Johnny nodded. "Damn, how much you find?"

"About four keys," Malone said.

"Leo's calling it in. Max is outside." Malone stepped into the stairway and turned to Johnny behind him. "You wanna look around just to be sure there isn't more shit stashed somewhere else in this joint?"

"Yeah, sure."

Max stood out front smoking a cigarette.

"Good day, huh?" Max said as Malone stepped through the doorway. Gunfire rang out from the front yard and Max fell to the ground in front of Malone. Malone immediately dove to the ground and drew his P226 and fired a burst in the direction of the oncoming gunfire. He then saw two shooters dressed in black and gold. Malone pulled the trigger again, hitting the shooter on the left in the head, and quickly fired several rounds toward the other on the right. Leo fired his Glock at the shooter, hitting him in the chest and sending him to the ground.

Malone got up to his feet and saw that both men were dead. Latin Kings. An eerie silence fell as he saw Max lying on the concrete. Malone swallowed hard as he saw blood spilling from his neck. He immediately crouched down and applied pressure to Max's neck as the snow on the ground turned red.

"Fucking shit—no—God no."

"We...g—got...em?" Max muffled through the blood in his throat.

"Yeah—we did buddy. Nailed the bastards. Just be quiet and fucking stay with me, okay? You hear me?"

Malone kept his hand over Max's neck and applied pressure.

Leo ran up and bent down by Malone and checked for a pulse on Max's wrist. Their eyes met. "The pulse is really weak," Leo said. "We need to get him out of the cold." Malone nodded and, together, they carried Max inside and put him on the couch.

Malone crouched down next to Max. "You're gonna be okay," he said. "Help's on the fucking way. You hear me?" Malone rubbed his eyes. A smear of blood spread on his face.

"Malone—" Max whispered

"Just be quiet. Save your energy. We're gonna get you fixed up, you hear me? Soon you'll be back at the bar shooting the shit."

Max smiled back at Malone and then his eyes glazed over.

"No—wait—no. Shit—no!" The color drained from Malone's face and he turned pale as he hunched over Max.

Leo crouched down and held Max's wrist, then his eyes met Malone's. "I—don't think I'm getting anything."

Malone watched as Leo started pushing down on Max's chest and counting aloud.

"One, two, three..."

"I'm not fucking giving up on you. You hear me? You're gonna be okay. You're gonna fucking be okay."

Max was still not responsive.

Leo kept doing CPR.

"Where's the fucking ambulance?" Malone barked.

"I don't know," Johnny said from the doorway.

A bead of sweat streamed down Leo's face as he continued CPR.

"Ambo's pulling up now," Johnny said.

Two EMTs entered the house with a stretcher.

"Sir? Sir? We need you to move."

Leo jerked his head up and got out of the way.

"You getting anything?" one EMT said to the other who was looking for a pulse.

Silence.

"Yeah—I—I got something. Really weak." The EMTs took Max out of the house and to the ambulance.

"Where you taking him?" Leo asked.

"Mercy," the EMT replied.

Malone took a deep breath as he watched the stretcher roll toward the flashing ambulance. He felt a burning sensation rise up his throat, bile about to come up. Malone looked away and stifled the urge with a cough.

"You want to ride with them?" Leo said as he wiped a bead of sweat with the back of his hand.

Malone continued to cough and shook his head. "I—gotta tell Jenna," he said as he got in his car. "Take her—to the —hospital."

"I'll go with 'em then," Leo said.

Malone didn't respond.

"Shouldn't we wait until backup arrives?" Johnny said.

"Yeah. Stay here," Leo said. "Then come to Mercy when you can."

Johnny nodded in agreement.

Malone glanced in the rearview mirror as he drove down the road and saw Johnny standing in the street. His eyes quickly moved away from the mirror and pulled out his flask.

As he turned onto Cicero, he took a drink. The street lights reflected on the windshield as the snow continued to fall. He wanted to close his eyes and pretend all of this was just a bad dream. Then he looked at his hands on the steering wheel and saw the bloodstains, reminding him that this nightmare was all too real. He took another drink until the whiskey started to calm his nerves. The urge to vomit was slowly numbed, a welcomed distraction as he sped down the road.

CHAPTER SEVEN

Malone pulled up in front of a brick house in the middle of a crowded neighborhood. He took another drink to push back the pain and anger. Then he slowly walked up the stairs and knocked on the door.

A brunette in her mid-thirties slowly opened the door. "Malone?" she said with a puzzled look.

"Yeah," Malone said in a quiet voice. "Can we talk?"

"Wait—where's Max? Where is he?"

Malone stepped forward to go inside but Jenna didn't move, causing him to stumble slightly. "Can I come in?"

She nodded and held the door open as Malone stepped inside. The living room was scattered with baby toys and an episode of Friends was on the TV in the corner.

"Look—uh—Max was just taken to Mercy Hospital."

Jenna's mouth hung open and the air left her lungs. She started gasping for breath and said, "No—no—."

"He got hit in the neck. Lost a lot of blood."

"Is—is he—?"

"He had a really weak pulse when EMS picked him up. I came here to take you to Mercy."

Jenna cupped her hands over her mouth and nose as tears streamed down her face.

Malone put his arms around her. "He's a tough bastard," he said. "You know that more than anyone. Let's go see how he's doing."

"Yeah. Yeah, he is. You're right."

Jenna put on her jacket and disappeared into the hallway. She had her son in her arms, wrapping him in a blanket.

"Take mine," Jenna said, handing Malone her keys. "We need the car seat."

"Right." Malone got in the driver's seat of the mini-van and started the ignition.

Malone quickly glanced and saw more tears pour down Jenna's face as she stared straight ahead.

"What the hell happened?" Jenna said quietly.

"We were coming out of a stash house, and there was two of 'em. Came outta nowhere. Then the ambulance came and took him to Mercy."

Malone noticed Jenna shaking and put his hand over her shoulder while keeping his eyes on the road.

"Hey—Leo was in the ambulance with Max. Let me call him."

Matthew started to cry in the backseat and Malone tried to block it out as he held the phone up to his ear.

"Shit! Fucking voicemail," Malone said loudly. "We'll be there in a minute."

Jenna didn't reply.

"He's a tough motherfucker. You know that. That fucker ain't goin nowhere."

Malone parked the mini-van by the entrance to the ER. Then Malone and Jenna walked into Mercy together.

Jenna cradled Matthew in her arms, holding him close. Johnny stood inside the sliding doors with a blank expression on his face.

"Any news?" Malone said.

"He's in the ICU. Leo's in the lobby with Carver."

Malone nodded.

Approaching the lobby, Malone saw Leo from a distance and noticed the bloodshot eyes.

Leo was too choked up to talk.

"What the fuck happened?" Malone said.

"He didn't make it," Leo finally said. "He lost too much blood. And he's gone."

The words cut through Malone as he stood there, frozen in place.

Jenna screamed out loud, waking her son who started to cry again.

Malone could hear the crying, but it felt far away and distant like he was somewhere else. He stood there silently as his eyes filled with tears.

Leo said something to Malone but the reality of Max's death drowned out the words. He could only stare back and not respond. Malone managed to walk over to a chair and sat down as tears continued to cloud his eyes. His eyes stuck to the floor as Carver walked over.

"Listen to me," Carver said. "It's not your fault."

Malone covered his face in the palms of his hands.

"Look at me—Malone." Carver got closer. "It's not your fault."

Malone slowly looked up. "No," he finally managed. "It is. It is. I'm the one who fucking took him in there."

"No. No, it's not," Carver said. "Listen to me. You're a good cop, but you don't know the future. Every day you've got a thousand assholes ready to take you out. You did your goddamn job. You hear me?"

Malone moved his eyes back to the floor and didn't say another word.

More officers came in and filled the lobby. Malone stayed

quiet and nodded at the sea of voices until they stopped talking. Someone gave him a flask, and he drank until he fell
asleep there in the chair. When he woke up, he had no idea
how much time had passed. Jenna was gone. Malone got up
and walked across the lobby to the bathroom.

As he stood at the urinal, questions flooded his mind:
What if he was the first one out of the house? What if he had
called for backup earlier? Countless other questions with no
definitive answers. Malone flushed and walked over to the
sink and turned on the water. He saw his reflection in the
mirror, blood had dried on his face. Max's blood. He let out a
growl and slammed his fist into the mirror. It cracked and
Malone's reflection became distorted. He screamed again and
hit the mirror again with his bloody fist. Malone took a
couple of steps back, saw his broken reflection, and collapsed
to the floor. He watched the fresh blood gather on his knuckles. The only sound in the room now was from the water
jetting down into the sink.

Leo walked into the bathroom and saw Malone on the
floor. Malone flinched back as Leo stepped toward him.

"It's okay," Leo said. "It's okay."

Malone didn't reply. He rubbed his eyes and buried his
face into his hands. "No," he finally said. "It's not okay. It's
any-fucking-thing but okay."

Leo sat next to Malone on the floor and didn't say
anything until another cop came into the bathroom. "Everything okay in here?"

"We're fine," Leo said. "Just give us a minute, okay?"

The officer shook his head and left. A few more minutes
passed before Malone spoke. "Guess hitting the mirror wasn't
the best idea, was it?"

Leo smiled. "No," he said. "It wasn't. Why don't we go get
that taken care of?"

"What the fuck happened?" Malone said.

"I think the shooters were coming back from the liquor store. Saw some full bottles of Jack in the yard."

Malone slowly leaned forward to get up.

"Here, let me help you," Leo offered. "Don't want to fuck up your hand any worse than it is."

Malone ignored Leo and groaned as he got up to his feet.

They walked out of the bathroom into the lobby, Malone's injured hand down by his side.

"Shit, you're still bleeding," Leo said. "I'll get you something for that."

"Oh fuck," Malone said, raising his hand and cradling it in his left. "Thanks."

Leo got some toilet paper and gave it to Malone. "I'll find someone to help with your hand."

Malone took a seat and wrapped his hand with the toilet paper. He drifted back in the chair and stared at the tiles on the ceiling.

Johnny came up to Malone. "Okay if I sit down?" he asked.

Malone shrugged.

Johnny brought him a cup of coffee in a small brown paper cup. Malone held it in his left hand, sipping it slowly. It tasted like shit, but at least it was warm. Something to help distract him from the pain.

"Is your hand okay?"

Malone turned towards him. "I'm fine," he said coldly.

"You sure? Looks like you're bleeding quite a bit there."

Malone nodded his head silently.

"I—uh—filed the report at the scene. They came in and took the heroin we found and put it in evidence."

Malone leaned forward in his seat. "Okay, that's good."

"They said it was over a hundred grand worth of heroin and twenty grand in cash. I could of swore there was more cash than that."

"I dunno. Good work. You—uh—seen Leo?"

"No, I haven't."

"Okay. Good work." Malone got up and walked out of the waiting room. He searched the hallway for Leo but only saw other cops, nurses, and staff. He finally found Leo sitting alone at a small table with a bag of chips.

Malone sat down at the table across from Leo.

"Hey," Leo said. "I found a nurse. Told her you were in the lobby."

"Okay." Malone leaned forward and said in a low voice, "Just remembered. Max put some cash in my trunk earlier tonight."

"Holy shit," Leo said.

"Yeah, I forgot about it."

Malone yawned.

"Your car here?"

"At Jenna's."

Leo nodded. "What are you thinking?"

"It's fine there," Malone said. "We can get it later."

"Yeah, you're right."

Malone pushed himself out of the chair and made his way back over to the lobby.

He heard a voice say, "Ryan Malone? You gotta be kidding me."

Malone turned around and smiled as he saw a familiar face: Morgan.

"Someone told me I need to help a cop with a banged-up hand and here you are," the nurse said.

"Hey Morgan," Malone said with as much energy as he could.

"I just heard about Max. I'm really sorry," Morgan said as she held her hand up to Malone's shoulder and gently squeezed it.

"Yeah," Malone said quietly.

"Why don't I take a look at that hand, huh? Take a seat."

Malone walked toward the corner of the lobby and sat down in an empty chair.

"Hell'd you do?" Morgan asked as she carefully pulled off the blood-soaked toilet paper.

"Bumped the mirror."

"Shit. Next time go for the heavy bag, ya know?"

"Yeah," Malone said quietly.

"Your entire hand is swollen. It's probably fractured. And you need stitches too. Let's get you down to X-ray."

"No, just wrap it up."

"You sure? I don't want to risk infection. And if it's fractured, it's gonna keep hurting like hell."

"I'm fine."

"If you say so," Morgan said.

"Really."

"I'm gonna go get some gauze and clean those cuts for you."

Malone nodded.

A couple of minutes later, Morgan came back, cleaned the hand, and wrapped it.

"This is not very official," she said. "You really need an X-ray."

"Got something for the pain?"

"This will help some." Morgan gave him two pills in a white paper medicine cup.

"Thanks."

"I'd love to tell you to rest, but I won't waste my breath. Take care of yourself, Malone."

"You too."

Malone watched Morgan walk away, yawned again, and rubbed his eyes. He wandered around the hospital and found Leo asleep in a chair.

Malone sat down next to Leo and yawned again. It woke Leo, his head jerking up to look around.

"Hey. Why don't we go now? Might even get to sleep in our own beds."

Leo yawned. "No," he said. "I'm okay. Just needed to close my eyes for a minute."

"Bullshit. I don't know what fucking time or day it is. It's time to go home. Anyone got a problem with that, fuck 'em."

Leo smiled. "Yeah, okay."

"Guess we can take a cab to Jenna's."

"Sure you're up for that?"

"Yep."

Leo and Malone walked out together from the hospital and Malone slowly lit a cigar as they stepped out into the dark parking lot.

"Everything's a fucking mess," Malone said.

"Yeah, it sure is."

"Maybe it's always been that way."

They were quiet during the cab ride until Leo said, "You stopping anywhere else tonight?"

Malone shook his head. "Nope. Just heading home."

"You sure?"

"Yeah."

"Alright."

Malone and Leo got out of the cab and walked over to Malone's black sedan.

The street was quiet and the sky was black. The snow on the ground glistened in the streetlights. The only sound was some dogs barking a block or two away.

Malone popped the trunk showing the black duffel bag inside. He unzipped it, revealing the stacks of cash.

"Max, you did it," Malone mumbled aloud.

"That's not bad at all," Leo said as Malone zipped the bag shut and closed the trunk.

"What do you want to do with it?" Leo asked as he opened the passenger door.

"Hookers and blow, right?" Malone said with a quiet laugh as he started the car.

Leo chuckled.

"Half to Jenna, and then we split it."

"Sounds good."

"I got a storage unit."

"In your name?"

"Yeah, got it when I moved out."

"You sure?"

"Just for a little while. Wanna swing by there tomorrow?"

Malone parked the car in the street in front of Leo's house.

"Yeah, let's do that." Leo got out of the car and stopped by the driver's door. Malone rolled down the window.

"Yeah?"

"You sure you're okay to drive?"

"Yeah. The painkillers are helping."

"That's good."

"We got some fucking work to do."

"Yeah," Leo said. "We sure do."

CHAPTER EIGHT

Malone woke up as sunlight blinded him through the window. Both his head and his hand hurt like hell. He held his hands up to provide relief from the light. Pain shot up and down his arm. Each movement required more effort than it should. He slowly rose out of bed and knocked over an empty whiskey bottle with his foot as he wandered over to the kitchen. He opened the freezer, and cringed as the cold air hit his face. He felt like shit before and now he felt worse.

He balanced a frozen bag of corn on his injured hand, pulled a bottle of aspirin from a drawer, and gulped a few down before taking a Budweiser from the fridge. As he drank it, the bag fell off of his injured hand.

"Shit!" he yelled. He set down the beer on the counter and picked up the corn. He stuck it under his armpit and pinned it there feeling the cold spread throughout his body as he took the beer over to the couch. He then noticed the black duffel bag on the floor next to the couch and slowly opened it, revealing the banded stacks of cash inside.

Malone gazed down at the cash, trying to remember what all happened the night before. He went into the bathroom and stood by the toilet. Still nothing. He couldn't remember anything clearly. "Motherfucker," Malone said out loud as he flushed the toilet. He turned on the shower, the hot water soothed the hangover and made him start to feel normal.

Suddenly, the images flashed in his mind.

Holding Max in his arms.

Driving Jenna to the hospital.

Shattering the mirror.

Feeling the pain in his bloody hands.

He turned off the water, picking a towel off the floor. Malone found a shirt, jeans, boxer shorts, and a pair of socks in a pile of clothes on top of his bed and got dressed. Once back in the living room, he looked down again at the bag of cash. His phone was next to the bag.

"Hey," Leo said as he answered Malone's call.

"Hey."

"You downtown?"

"No."

"Weren't you picking me up for an errand?"

"Oh, yeah," Malone said. "I'm on my way,"

"Okay."

Malone took a slice of leftover pizza from the fridge and carefully filled his flask with whiskey and took a drink. Then he slung the black bag over his shoulder and slowly closed the door. Once inside his car, he bumped his injured hand on the seatbelt as he sat down.

"Shit! Shit. Shit."

He sighed and awkwardly reached across his body to buckle up with his left hand. He growled as pain shot up and down his hand toward his elbow as he turned the key. He then reached down and shifted the car into drive.

Leo was waiting outside when Malone pulled up in front of the house. "How you feeling?" he asked as he got in.

"Like dog shit," Malone said. "You?"

"I hear you. I'm not too bad. How's the hand?"

"Eh, I'll survive. Storage unit is by Mag Mile."

"In your name?'

"Yeah. Got it when I moved out about six months ago."

"How's security?"

"Got a few cameras. Need a code to get in. Just a key to open the unit."

"You having any second thoughts about this?"

"Not at all," Malone said. "You?"

"Nope."

"Good. There are some hats we can wear in the backseat."

Leo reached back and put on a black White Sox hat and gave Malone the red Bulls hat.

"You know those assholes cost me a fortune this year," Malone said as he parked next to the brick building.

"I believe you. That's why I prefer mutual funds."

Malone took a pull from his flask and tossed it back inside the glove box.

"Grab the bag, will ya?"

"Sure."

Leo picked up the black bag and followed Malone through a set of glass doors.

Malone pulled his hat low, blocking most of his face.

Leo did the same.

Together they moved past a few storage units on both sides and stood together waiting for the elevator.

"Got quite a few cameras here," Leo said quietly.

"Yeah, they do."

Malone entered the elevator and saw his reflection on the silver wall. He looked like shit. He immediately shifted his eyes away and the elevator opened on the third floor. Malone got out and walked to the right and Leo followed. He stopped at the end of the hallway, turned, kneeled down, and unlocked the orange, metal garage-like door at the floor.

Malone slowly raised the door, clacking as it went up. The small cage was filled with brown cardboard boxes and plastic bins stacked halfway to the ceiling. Leo followed Malone inside.

Malone led Leo through piles of boxes. He pointed to the stack of plastic storage bins toward the bottom of a stack of boxes.

"Thinking one of these bins would probably work," he said.

"You have anything more secure than that?"

"Nope. We can get a safe but have to bring it in here."

Leo nodded. "Yeah. I guess that works for now."

Leo put the duffel bag inside the bin and closed the lid, then he stacked three more bins on top.

"Okay, let's get out of here and head downtown," Malone said.

They walked outside and approached Malone's car. "Let me drive," Leo said. "I heard you making noises when you bumped your hand inside a minute ago."

"No, no. I'm fine."

Once inside police headquarters, Malone walked by the front desk and Leo followed close behind.

"Heard from Johnny?"

"Nope. Maybe he's in the office," Leo replied.

"Yeah. I'm gonna get some coffee," Malone said.

Malone poured a cup of coffee in the empty break room and saw Carver in the doorway.

"Malone," Carver said. "My office."

Malone nodded and followed Carver into his office, then sat down in one of two small black chairs facing the paper-covered desk. Malone set down his coffee.

"Surprised you're in today," Carver said.

"Really? I got some work to do."

"Don't overdo it, huh? You need to talk to someone about Max."

Malone felt a sour taste in his mouth as he looked over at the framed photo of a policeman on the wall and then his eyes met Carver's.

"Yeah, I guess you're right."

"I'm really sorry about what happened. First your nephew and now this? Total bullshit."

"Sure is," Malone said as his eyes bounced back to the wall.

"Wish I had some good news for you, but I don't. There's gonna be an investigation into Max. IAD."

"You fucking kidding me? What's there to investigate? We were ambushed outside of a goddamn stash house."

"I know. I know. It's bullshit. IAD's got a stick up their ass and wanna make sure you did it by the book."

"I fucking did. This is fucking bullshit! He ain't even been fucking buried yet." Malone threw his mug against the wall and a stream of coffee flew through the air. Ceramic pieces scattered across the room.

Carver jumped out of his chair.

"Fucking shit, Malone!"

"This is bullshit! We just lost a good fucking cop, and now the rats are up our ass?"

Carver sat down in the chair next to Malone and put his arm around him.

"I know. I know. I agree with you. It's total bullshit. But we can't fight them. We do, and it looks like we're hiding something. You know there's a long list of assholes who want both of our badges. So just put a nice shit-eating grin on your face for the stupid pricks."

"Want me to bend over too?"

"Feels like it, doesn't it?" Carver said with a slight smile. "Just do whatever they ask. And don't give 'em any shit."

Malone put his hands on his face and slowly moved them down to the stubble on his jawline and put his hands back on his lap.

"A goddamn fucking dog and pony show."

"Exactly. And you don't have to like it," Carver said as he walked back around to his desk. "Go home. Get some rest. Come back in a few days."

Malone got up from his chair.

"Sorry about the mess."

"It's alright. Need to clean in here anyway."

Malone turned to walk out.

"Malone?"

"Yeah."

"You found over 100 grand in heroin during that bust. That's a lot of shit that won't be hitting the streets."

"Yeah, sure," Malone said as he opened the door.

"What's your next move?"

"Keep digging into the Latin Kings."

"Anything there?"

"Working on that today."

"Okay. Keep me in the loop. Got it?"

"Yeah."

Malone left Carver's office and got some more coffee. At the end of the hall, he entered the office with the unmarked door and saw Leo sitting at a desk, staring at the computer.

"Where the hell is Johnny?" Malone said as he sat down at his desk in the middle of the room. He glanced over and saw Max's desk and felt an empty sinking sensation in his gut and quickly moved his eyes away.

"I'm not sure. No messages or anything. Maybe you should give him a call."

"Yeah. Carver says the rats are investigating what happened."

"What's there to investigate?"

"I know," Malone said. "It's fucked up."

"Any idea when?"

"Didn't say. Probably pretty soon." Malone took a sip of coffee. "What were you looking at?"

"The intel we have on the Latin Kings."

"Good. Any new leads?"

"Not yet."

Malone picked up the phone and called Johnny but got his voicemail after four rings.

"Hey. Where the hell are you? Call me back."

Malone paced around the office, looking at pictures of known suspects posted on the wall as Leo typed on the computer.

"Hey," Malone said.

Leo looked up from his computer.

"Was he shaken up yesterday?"

"Yeah, he was. Said that he's never shot anyone before."

Malone took another sip of coffee. "Okay. I'm gonna go check on him."

Leo's eyes flicked back to his computer screen. "Sure," he said.

"Lemme know if you find anything. And send me Johnny's address, will ya?"

"Will do."

Malone noticed Johnny's black Jeep parked on the street. He got out of the car and knocked on the door. Johnny came to the door wearing jeans and a grey hoodie. Malone remembered they were the same clothes he had on yesterday.

"We need to talk. You gonna let me in?"

"Yeah, yeah. Sorry. I was on my way in and..."

Johnny held the door open and Malone stepped inside and stood in the doorway. He could smell the beer on Johnny's breath.

"Look, it was a really fucked up day," Malone said. "Shit went really fucking bad. But I need to know if you're gonna be able to work."

"I—I—uhh," Johnny's voice cracked. He sat back down on the couch and buried his face in his hands. "I fucked up. It's my fault."

Malone said as he sat down on the couch next to Johnny, "What the hell are you talking about?"

"I was upstairs when I—uh—heard the gunfire."

"Yeah."

"It's on me. It's my fault Max got killed."

"That's bullshit," Malone said. "We were fucking ambushed. Don't put this shit on yourself."

"I should've had your back. I should've been there with you. I should've..."

"I told you to go back and look for more shit. You followed orders. So shut the fuck up about not having our backs. You hear me?"

"Yeah. I hear ya."

"Look, you're gonna be fine. You hear me? Rest up. Get your shit together. Come back tomorrow."

Malone stood up and walked to the door and Johnny followed.

"You're gonna be fine. You hear me?"

"Yeah, I do," Johnny said.

Malone left the house and took a drink from his flask as he got in his car. He looked in the rearview mirror, the dark circles under his eyes staring back at him. He moved his eyes to the road as he started the car.

Malone turned on South Halstead and got stuck in traffic. He hated traffic with a passion. He tapped his hands on the steering wheel as he waited then looked over at the passenger seat and imagined Max sitting there.

"Turn on the fucking light, man. Can't do shit if we're stuck here with our thumbs up our asses." Malone could still hear the words Max said a few days ago ringing out in his head.

He turned on the radio and flipped through a few channels. All commercials. He turned the radio off. A blue minivan drove past on his left and Malone watched it. It looked just like Ann's. Malone sped up and looked inside to see a woman with curly blonde hair. He took a deep breath and looked back up at the light ahead. It was green, but none of the cars ahead were moving. He reached into his jacket and pulled out the flask again and took another drink.

"Bout fucking time," he said aloud as the cars began inching forward.

He could still hear Max's voice in his head as he drove down the street. He turned the radio back on to tune out his thoughts. He took another drink, put his flask back in the glovebox, and went into the station.

Ramirez from Narcotics approached Malone as he saw him in the hallway. "Hey Malone, what's new with you?"

"Hey. You know how it goes. Just stirring up shit. Happens a lot when the gig is playing with assholes."

"Good thing there's no shortage," Ramirez said with a laugh.

"Ain't that the truth."

"What you got going?"

"Just picked up a kid for slinging at the corner of 88th and Commercial. Right by a church and a school. Looks like it's gang-related. He was wearing Latin King colors."

"No shit. Got a name?"

"José Díaz. Think you got anything on him?"

"Let's go see."

The two men entered the GTF office and startled Leo as they entered.

"Hey. Can you look up a José Díaz?" Malone said to Leo.

"He has a possible Latin King connection," Ramirez said.

Leo typed into the computer and stared at the screen before saying anything else. "Okay, not too much on him. Wait a second—looks like he's the nephew of Juan Cruz. Got an outstanding warrant out on Juan."

"We picked up this kid on a drug charge at 88th and Commercial," Ramirez said. Malone looked at the map on the wall.

"That's Disciple turf," he said. "Kings must be branching out."

"Or this kid ain't very bright," Ramirez said.

"This kid's gonna skate. No priors, right?"

"Nope."

"Then why don't we get something useful out of him?" Malone said.

Ramirez leaned forward in his seat. "What you thinking?"

"You got him selling by a school, right?"

"Yeah."

"Stash house can't be too far away then."

"Yeah, probably not."

"Why not cut 'em loose and tail him?"

"Yeah," Ramirez said. "You're right. That's a good idea."

Malone turned toward Leo.

"So much for today being quiet," Leo said.

CHAPTER NINE

Malone and Ramirez sat inside a vacant warehouse staring out the window. "I can't believe the little prick went right back slinging on the corner," Ramirez said.

"Really? I ain't surprised in the least."

"No matter what, you owe me one," Ramirez said. "I think my ass is frozen solid. We been here all day just watching and waiting."

"I hear you," Malone said as he set down a white styro-foam coffee cup. "But remember, this shit bird could lead us to an even bigger shit bird."

"This is true."

Malone took a sip of cold black coffee and wiped his mouth with the back of his hand.

"Thanks for letting us borrow the bug from Narcotics."

"Just gotta make sure it makes its way back in one piece."

"Don't sweat it."

Across the street, José left his corner and went down a back alley.

"Shit," Malone said. "I'm gonna trail the kid. Might be a re-up. Keep an eye out here."

"Will do."

Malone ran down the concrete stairs, then briskly walked across the street. He picked up his pace once he got to the alley, searching for any sign of the kid. Nothing.

"Shit," he whispered to himself.

He followed the alley to the other end on 87th Street, where he saw the kid go into a corner store. He watched the door for a few minutes but the kid didn't come out. Taking a deep breath, Malone crossed the street and went inside. As he strolled down the aisles, he picked up a bag of chips. Round mirrors by the ceiling let him scan the place. The kid was nowhere to be found. Probably in the backroom. Malone saw the closed door to the backroom. He walked over to it and pulled on it. Locked.

Malone approached the front counter where a thirty-something woman stood by the register.

"Where is the bathroom?" he asked.

"No hay uno," the woman said, shaking her head. "Lo siento."

"Bien," Malone said. He paid for the chips and left.

"I lost the damn kid," Malone said into his phone as he started walking back down the dark alley, crunching a chip in his mouth.

"It's okay," Ramirez said. "I was just going to call you."

"Huh?"

"A dark SUV stopped at the corner while you were chasing the kid. A guy came out to the vehicle and said a new shipment's coming in tomorrow night at 9. Warehouse on South Halstead."

"You fucking kidding me?"

"Nope. This is the real deal."

"About time we got some good news," Malone said with a wide smile.

Minutes later, Malone stormed into the GTF office causing Leo to flinch behind his desk.

"You ain't gonna believe this," Malone announced.

"Why? What do you have?"

"Got a delivery tomorrow night at 9. Warehouse on South Halstead."

"How'd you get it?"

"Bug on the street. It worked like a charm," Ramirez said. "Like they said it right in front of me, plain as day."

Leo laughed. "Holy shit."

"Do me a favor?" Malone asked. "Don't run this up the ladder. Don't want any higher ups sticking their nose in this."

"No problem," Ramirez said. "I get it."

Ramirez left the room and Malone looked over at Leo. He shook his head in disbelief.

"I can't believe this shit," Malone said.

"Yeah, me either."

"Why don't we go take a look at this place, get a feel for the layout?"

"Yeah, good idea."

"I'm gonna grab some coffee, hit the john. I'll meet you by my car."

"Alright."

Malone came out of the building with a cup of coffee in each hand.

"Your hand feeling any better?" Leo asked.

"Yeah, it is," Malone said, holding out the other coffee. "Just a little sore."

"Glad to hear it," Leo said as he took a sip. "I think coffee at the station is getting worse."

"Guess it's better than nothing."

"If you say so."

"I told Carver about our tip," Malone commented. "He's as excited as you and me."

"I bet."

They got into the car. The wipers cleared the snow off the windshield.

"Hopefully Ramirez can join us tomorrow night. If not, at least Johnny's back tomorrow."

"Yeah, but is he ready?"

Malone sighed and started the car. "Good question. He better be."

"Your heat not work?"

"It works when it wants to work. Kinda like a fucking politician," Malone said.

Leo laughed.

"Think there's an extra pair of gloves in the backseat."

Leo searched for a pair of gloves in the backseat.

"It's a weird day, ain't it?" Malone said.

"What do you mean?"

"I don't know. Like the day's in slow motion. It's really weird."

"Yeah, I guess you're right."

Malone took another sip. "Okay, you're right, this coffee really is shit." He poured the cup of coffee out the window.

"I can't find any gloves."

"Maybe in the glovebox?"

The sunlight reflected off of the snow and ice on the ground, blinding Malone as he peered through the windshield to the street ahead.

"See if there's any sunglasses in there too," Malone said. "I can't see a damn thing."

"Don't see any sunglasses," Leo said as he rifled through the glovebox. "But I did find some gloves. What the hell is this?" Leo held up a glow-in-the-dark condom sealed in its package.

Malone laughed and it quickly evolved into a sigh. "That crazy son of a bitch. A few weeks ago, he was ranting about glow-in-the-dark condoms. He mentioned that he was gonna get me some. No idea he put that in there."

Leo shook his head in disbelief and smiled. "Anything you guys didn't talk about?"

"Everything was pretty much fair game."

Malone pulled in front of the donut shop. "Figure we can get some coffee that doesn't taste like shit and then hike it from here to the warehouse."

Malone and Leo went into the donut shop and greeted a middle-aged blonde at the counter.

"Two large black coffees," Malone said. He turned to Leo. "Want anything else? My treat."

"Just coffee."

The woman handed over two large Styrofoam cups. "On the house, boys."

"Thanks," Leo said.

"Yeah, thanks."

Once outside and walking down the sidewalk, Leo asked, "They said the delivery would be at 9 tomorrow night?"

"Yeah, that's right," Malone said. "Ramirez said they'd give us some support tomorrow night. Figure that means one, two guys. That's four, maybe even five of us with Johnny."

"Okay. Good to know," Leo said.

As they got a block away from the building, Malone stopped and held his hand up briefly. "Let's hang here for a minute, see what we can see." He sipped his coffee.

"Going from the photos, there's a parking lot right next to the building," Leo said. "That's where they'd get deliveries."

"Sure. Any known video cameras at the facility?"

"Couldn't tell anything from the records."

"We'll have to take a closer look then," Malone said. "Wanna split up and I'll pick you up in a minute?"

"Yeah, fine."

Malone bit his lip and stared down at the sidewalk as he walked down South Halstead. He looked up. About a block over was a long row of houses on South Emerald. Houses full of families. Even though police headquarters were just about a mile down the road, no one could do a damn thing about the drugs taking over the city, like a cancer.

Malone walked in front of a bakery and saw the reflection of a black Cadillac rolling to a stop. A tight feeling in his gut. It reminded him of when he got shot a few years ago in the shoulder. A Vice Lord's initiation. Fire a few rounds at a cop. Malone put his hand inside his jacket, ready to draw from his shoulder holster. He sped up his stride, just a few feet from his car. He heard a car door fling open as he climbed into his car. He flicked his eyes to the rearview mirror to see a young black woman get out of the car and walk into the bakery. He took a deep breath and stared as his reflection in the mirror while he took a long drink from his flask. Then he called Leo.

"What'd you find out?" Malone asked.

"Didn't see any noticeable security cameras around the perimeter. Six cars in the parking lot next to the building."

"Okay good. How's visibility? Figure the delivery will be with a van or truck."

"Not great. We'll probably have to get creative."

"Okay. Maybe a spotter in the parking lot and the rest on the other side of the building." Malone said.

"Yeah, makes sense."

"Okay, I'm gonna come pick you up."

Malone pulled up and Leo got in. "So now the heat works?"

"Told you it works when it wants to."

"You weren't kidding."

They drove past McFadden's Irish Pub. "Why don't we go get a taste?" Malone asked.

"Yeah," Leo said. "But let's only have one drink."

It was mostly empty inside of McFadden's. There were just a few people sitting at the bar. Malone and Leo sat down at the end of the bar. Malone made eye contact with the older male bartender. "What'll it be?" he asked them.

"Four shots of Jameson," Malone said.

"I'll take a Bud Light," Leo added.

The bartender walked back to the other end to get the drinks.

"You come here often?" Leo said.

"We'd hit this place a few times," Malone said. "Max always preferred the strip joints. I liked the bars better. We'd mix it up some."

The bartender delivered their drinks.

Malone quickly gulped down his first shot.

Leo took a swig of his beer and said, "I can't believe he's gone. You talked to Jenna?"

"No, I haven't. But we got that gift for her."

"We sure do," Leo said as he took another swig of beer.

"And we gotta get the fucking pricks that did this and start cleaning up this town," Malone replied.

Leo smiled and held up his beer for a toast.

"I'll drink to that."

Malone held up his second shot.

"To CPD," they both said as their glasses clinked.

"And fuck the fuckers that stand in our way," Malone added.

Leo raised his beer again.

Both men took a drink.

"We better stop now, we can't overdo it."

Malone pushed a shot over in front of Leo. "To Max," Malone said as he raised up his third shot.

Leo shrugged slightly and then picked up a glass. "To Max," he said.

They swallowed their shots.

Leo looked down at his watch. "I gotta use the restroom and we can get back to it."

"Yeah, okay."

Leo came back to find another round of shots in front of his seat.

"To Max's family," Malone held up another glass.

Leo sighed and sat down. "You sure about this? We got more work to do. And Carver will hit the fan if..."

"What would Max want?" Malone said.

"Yeah, I guess you're right."

Leo picked up the glass. "To Max's family," he said.

CHAPTER TEN

Malone woke up in the dark with his head pounding, not sure where he was. He reached to his left and felt the worn fabric on his couch. The faint smell of cigar smoke. He wasn't sure how he'd gotten home. The last thing he remembered was throwing back shots with Leo. The rest of the night was a memory that had already faded away.

"Motherfucker," Malone said as he leaned forward. He put his feet over the side of the bed and stood up, stepping in vomit. He wiped off his feet with a towel, swallowed a few aspirin, dropped the towel on the vomit and laid down again on the bed.

He woke about an hour later to the sound of knocking on the door.

"Ugh. Go the fuck way," he mumbled. The pounding continued as he slowly got out of bed in his underwear and his foot squished on the vomit-soaked towel. "Son of a bitch," he said as the towel moved under his foot. He looked through the peep hole to see an attractive brunette in her early thirties—Ann. She had on a blue winter jacket, dark jeans and brown boots. She was standing next to a young boy bundled up in a puffy red winter coat. James. Malone took a deep breath and opened the door a few inches. "Hey, one second," he said. "Be right there." He slipped on a pair of jeans, put a shirt on, and ran his hand under the faucet and splashed the water on his hair and went to the door.

"Hi. I just got out of the shower," Malone said as he opened the door slightly. He looked down at the boy. "Hey, how you doing, buddy?"

The boy smiled. "Look Dad," he said, a red pickup truck in his hand.

"That's great. Mom get you that?"

"Yeah! And we're goin' to the zoo today!"

Malone covered his open mouth, his eyes wide.

"Why aren't you ready?" Ann asked as she crossed her arms. "You said you put it on your calendar. Didn't you remember? He's so excited."

"I need to talk to you for a minute," Malone said.

Ann nodded her head slowly and crossed her arms. "James, why don't you play with your truck over by the sidewalk?"

James quickly ran over with his red truck in his hand.

Ann glared at Malone. "I can't believe you. You're drunk aren't you?"

"No," Malone lowered his voice. "No. But I had a rough night."

"What else is new? You'd rather get wasted and screw some skank than spend time with your son."

"Max—he—got shot a couple days ago. Didn't make it. I went out with the team last night and had a few drinks but didn't get drunk."

Anne exhaled loudly. "Oh no!" she said as she put her arms around Malone and hugged him. "I'm so sorry. I know what he meant to you."

She smelled the alcohol on his breath and felt like she'd been punched in the stomach.

"Yeah. I'm doing alright," Malone's voice cracked. He covered his hand to cover the cough.

"Why the hell can't you pick up the damn phone?" she asked. "Just put down the bottle for once and say something to someone."

"You're right," he said. "I should have called you."

Malone looked down at his feet.

"You going to talk to anyone about it?"

"You know I can't—"

"Oh yeah, that's right. Cops just hold in everything. Drink your problems away. How's that working for you?"

"That's bullshit," Malone said, his voice raised. He lowered it back down. "Let's talk later, okay? I mean it, Ann. I'll call you, okay?"

Ann turned around and walked over to James. Malone followed with her. "Get your shit together," Ann said. "James misses you. He needs his father."

"Yeah, I will—yeah."

"Okay, let's go to the zoo. Dad's staying home."

"Aww. Dad? You're not going?"

"Sorry pal, I'm not feeling too good."

"You sure you can't come?"

"No, not today, buddy."

"Aww, come on," James said as tears were forming in his eyes.

"See ya, buddy," Malone said as he waved, his voice trailing off. "I'll see ya." He sat there watching as they got into the minivan and left. He waved again, but this time James didn't wave back. He walked back into his apartment and laid down on the couch, listening to the voices of a sitcom on the TV in the dark room.

A couple hours later, Malone woke up to the sound of his phone ringing.

"Huh?" he said into the phone. "What?"

"Malone? Where the hell are you? Get your ass down here."

"Yes, sir. Sorry. I'll be there in just a few minutes."

Malone slowly got up from the couch, popped a few aspirin and got dressed. He looked at the cabinet, thought about getting a drink and then opened the fridge, finding it empty other than some eggs and old pizza.

"Motherfucker," Malone mumbled under his breath. He'd been living off of coffee, donuts and whiskey. He shook his head in disgust, took a bottle of whiskey from a cabinet, and pulled the flask from his jacket. Then he grabbed the funnel from on top of the refrigerator and filled the flask. Malone then took a quick drink from the bottle and put it back in the cabinet.

The bright sunlight coming in through the windows at the station made him want to hide and go back to his apartment. The break room was empty aside from half a cup of luke-warm bitter coffee in the pot. Malone took it anyway, sipped it, and knocked on Carver's door. Carver waved him in.

"You look like shit, Malone."

"Nice to see you too," Malone said under his breath.

"What's that?"

"Just been a rough couple days."

"For sure. A real shit storm."

Carver got up from his chair and started to pace around his office.

"Look," he said. "I'm giving you some slack here. A helluva lot of slack. Just be straight with me. We lost a good man and a damn good cop, too. Where the hell you been? You living in the bottom of a whiskey bottle or what?"

Malone bit his lip. "I can't believe he's gone," he managed.

"You gotta do better than this. Sober up. You're a sergeant. You've got a team with others looking up to you."

"Yeah, you're right."

"I just heard that you got a lead on a shipment coming in later today."

"Yeah." Malone leaned forward in his chair. "Tonight at 9."

"You up for it? You're hungover and looking like a pile of shit that's been stepped on several times."

"I'm fine. I just gotta get back on the job. I'm good."

"You sure?"

"Yeah, absolutely."

"Get sobered up before you do anything, got it?"

"Will do."

"I know you were talking to Narcotics about helping out tonight, but they got pulled in on another job. That gonna be a problem?"

"No, we'll be fine."

"Alright then. Go get 'em."

Malone got up from the chair and strolled into the GTF office. Leo was typing while Johnny drank coffee by a whiteboard.

"Find out anything new for tonight?" Malone asked.

"Nope. Thinking a delivery truck or a moving van for tonight's delivery," Leo said.

"Agreed," Malone said as he looked over at Johnny still sipping his coffee.

Johnny put down his mug when he saw Malone's eyes on him.

Malone smiled and looked back over at Leo.

"We're flying solo tonight," Malone said. "Narcotics got pulled into something else."

Leo pulled up an image of the brick building on his computer.

"Okay, this is the only easy access point," he said. "Then you have that gated parking lot with the loading docks to the side here."

"Yeah. So one spotter in each direction and another waiting in the parking lot out of sight."

"Makes sense."

"The spotters close in once we get confirmation," Malone said.

"Yeah. What if there is more than one vehicle or some backup?" Leo asked.

"Doubtful," Malone said. "That's more risk. These guys are careful. If two come in, we'll improvise."

"You sure we can't ask someone else for some help?" Johnny asked.

Malone turned and leaned toward Johnny. "We fucking got this, you hear me? Let's do our damn job."

"Alright," Johnny said, nervously nodding back at Malone.

Malone took a sip of coffee and exhaled.

"Let's get ready and roll out in thirty," he said. "We're gonna find out more in the field than we will second guessing ourselves here."

Both Leo and Johnny nodded in agreement.

All three men went to the locker room. Johnny pulled out an extra pair of socks. Malone saw Johnny putting them on. "Good idea," he said. "Got your diaper?"

"Oh yeah, already got one on," Johnny said with a laugh.

"Still think I'm kidding about that story, huh?"

"No, I believe you."

Malone smiled back and raised his eyebrows. "Just don't shit or piss yourself in my car, okay?"

Leo stifled his laughter by holding his hand to his face and scratching under his nose.

Malone slipped his vest over his head and tightened it, realizing that Max was in his arms the last time he wore it.

His eyes moved toward Max's locker right next to his. He held out his hand toward it, but pulled back and slipped his hand inside his vest. He looked over at Johnny now wore his vest as well.

"You good?"

"Yeah," Johnny said as sweat glistened on his forehead.

"Good. Wanna drive the van and follow me?"

"Sure, I can drive."

Malone handed Johnny the keys, then he and Leo got into the snow-covered Chevy Impala.

Malone's eyes moved toward the rearview mirror as he drove ahead of Johnny in the van.

"How you feeling about this deal tonight?" Malone said.

"Not too sure," Leo said. "A mix of good, bad, and whatever else is in between."

"Yeah, I hear that. I'm not too sure either." He paused. "It's fucked up."

"It is indeed."

"I'm putting Johnny on the sidelines as much as possible tonight," Malone said. "Just harder with a goddamn crew of three."

"Sure is. So he's a spotter?"

"Yeah, but I'm gonna put him with you. You'll be on the far East corner. I'll be in the parking lot."

"Got it."

Malone pulled his flask out of his pocket.

"You sure about that?" Leo said.

"Sure as shit."

"Just don't overdo it, okay?"

"Fuck," Malone grumbled. "You sound like my ex, you know?"

Malone took a slow drink and put the flask down.

"Sorry, just—I want you to keep a clear head."

"I'll keep it under control, alright?"

"Okay."

"I'd worry about the guy behind us more than me," Malone said under his breath.

"What's that?" Leo said.

"Maybe we should get something to eat, maybe a cup of coffee before we stand around freezing our asses off, huh?"

"Yeah, good idea."

———

Malone and Leo walked into the donut shop and shook off the cold as they kicked their boots on a black mat by the door.

"I'll be right back," Leo said as he walked to the restroom.

Malone ordered coffee and a plain bagel. He then heard the door open behind him.

Johnny walked in.

"What do you want?" Malone asked.

"You paying?"

"Yeah, sure."

"Thanks."

Johnny ordered coffee and a glazed donut at the counter.

Malone paid and asked, "Where's Leo?"

"In the can, I guess," Johnny said.

"Gotcha."

"How you feeling about tonight?"

"Good. Ready to get back into action."

Malone sipped his coffee. "You can drop the act, kid. It's normal to be scared. Every day we're diving headfirst into a shitstorm."

Johnny nodded.

"You getting some sleep?"

"Yeah, some."

"Over five hours a night?"

"Around that."

"Don't you fucking lie to me. I can tell. At least four hours?"

"Yeah, right around there."

"Okay. Be straight with me. Got it?"

"Yeah, of course."

Malone pulled a cigar from his pocket and put it in his mouth. "Gonna go smoke outside. Be back in a minute."

Once outside, Malone lit his cigar while watching the snow-covered cars move down the road. He pulled the cigar out of his mouth and puffed smoke into the air. Then he pulled out his phone and saw a message from Ann.

"Call me when you can," she had said.

Malone put the phone back in his pocket and continued to smoke his cigar. He tried to soak in the city's silence since these moments were few and far between. He stubbed out his cigar in the ashtray by the door and sat down at a table across from Leo and Johnny as they ate their donuts. Malone smiled.

"Looks like you're enjoying yourselves." Malone leaned over and said quietly, "You got some chocolate on your face, man."

"Oh, thanks," Leo said as he wiped his face with a napkin and took another bite.

Malone sipped his coffee again. "We'll head out in a few minutes," he said as he took a bite of his bagel.

"Okay, I'm gonna get something for the road," Leo said and then went up to the counter.

Johnny finished his donut and wiped his hands. "Okay, I'm gonna go to the restroom," Johnny said.

Malone nodded and tapped his fingers on the table like he was playing the drums.

Leo came back to the table with coffee in one hand and a white bag in the other. "Just in case this takes a while," Leo said.

"Yeah, right," Malone said with a yawn.

"How's he seem to you?" Leo said.

"Think he's just a bit nervous," Malone said. "He'll be okay. How are you?"

"I'm good."

"You sure? You look a little nervous too," Malone said as he pulled his flask out of his jacket. "Want a taste? It'll calm those nerves."

"Yeah. Thanks." Leo took the flask and poured some into his coffee cup and handed it back to Malone. "You're figuring one or two delivery guys and a few more at the warehouse?" he asked

"Yeah. Sounds about right. Be surprised if any more than that."

The two men sat in silence until Johnny came back to the table.

Malone stood up and then Leo followed. "Okay boys, time to go to work."

CHAPTER ELEVEN

Malone stepped out of the car and the frigid air hit his face. Leo zipped his coat all the way up over his mouth. Johnny had his stocking hat pulled down near his eyes.

"Damn, Ramirez is missing all the fun, ain't he?" Malone said, his breath clouding the air.

"Sure is," Leo said.

"I'll hang by the side parking lot, and you two take the side street on the east side," Malone said.

"What if you need help?" Johnny asked.

"I'll be out of sight. They come out, I fall back. It's that simple."

"You sure?" Johnny said.

"Yeah. No time to argue over this shit right now. We need to get in position."

Johnny stared at Malone and then followed Leo to the east side of the building. Malone went around to the front of the warehouse and kneeled down next to a white delivery van.

He stayed in position for a few minutes, trying to ignore the cold by using box breathing. Inhale. Hold. Exhale. Hold.

Repeat. It seemed to help him stay more focused on the task at hand.

He pulled out his flask and the whiskey warmed his throat. He checked his watch; fifteen minutes had passed. He put his flask back into his jacket as he saw the headlights of a truck driving down the road: a U-Haul truck. Malone drew his P226 from his shoulder holster as the truck pulled up next to the warehouse. "This U-Haul appears to be the delivery vehicle," Malone said into his radio. "Start coming around."

A twenty-something Hispanic man got out of the truck, walked around to the back, and pulled up the sliding back door. No gun visible. Four Hispanic men came out of the warehouse, all dressed in black and yellow. Three appeared to have guns and one held a black bag.

Malone got a better angle of the men walking out. Two had handguns and the other one had a shotgun. Malone radioed to Johnny and Leo, "Hurry, it's going down right now."

Malone's attention went back to the U-Haul driver and the four Latin Kings standing in front of him. He couldn't hear what they were saying from the distance, so he stayed low and got closer, finding cover near a black Mercedes SUV.

The driver opened the back of the U-haul and disappeared inside.

A voice said something inside the back of the truck but Malone couldn't make it out. The driver reappeared with a similar black bag. The driver opened it up, the other man nodded and handed over his bag.

"CPD—freeze!" Malone barked. "Drop your weapons!" The man with the shotgun aimed it at Malone. "Last chance, asshole!" Malone screamed. A fraction of a second later, the man fired the shotgun, causing Malone to hide behind the Mercedes. Malone stayed crouched down and carefully moved toward the front of the vehicle, firing his P226 and hitting the gunman in the chest with the first shot. The second shot caught the gunman in the neck and dropped him to the ground. The shooter laid there, motionless in the snow. Malone couldn't tell if he was dead or not but knew he was no longer a problem. One of the men with a revolver returned fire at Malone and he quickly took cover again. The sound of the firing revolver filled the air. Malone kept low while he waited for a break in the gunfire.

Leo and Johnny appeared with their Glocks drawn. "Freeze!" Leo yelled. "Drop it!" The two other men turned toward Johnny and Leo. Johnny fired a couple rounds, but missed wide. Leo fired a burst, taking out one of the men and sending him to the ground. The other Latin King with the revolver fired at Leo but missed as he took cover behind a dumpster.

Malone waited for the man to pop up and shot the man in the chest, causing him to drop the revolver as he tumbled to the ground. Malone shifted his attention to the driver who was running to the cab of the U-Haul. "Get the one with the cash," Malone ordered to the others. "I got the driver." Malone locked in on the driver and stopped him just outside the door.

"Freeze! Drop it! Get on the ground! Hands behind your head!" The man didn't move, just stared at the driver's door as held the black bag. "Hear me, asshole? Drop it and get on the ground."

The driver dropped the bag by his feet and Malone thought he saw the man reach for something. "Freeze motherfucker," Malone ordered. "Put your hands on your head." Malone saw the driver had something in his hand and Malone fired his P226 and took the man down with several rounds in the back.

Malone kneeled down and found a grenade in the dead man's hand. "Stupid asshole," Malone said.

"You okay?" Leo said.

"Yeah." Malone took a deep breath. "I'm good."

"What the hell happened?"

"Told the pricks to freeze and they started firing at me. Thankfully, they're all lousy shots. Then this asshole here tried tossing this at me." Malone pointed toward the grenade. "Stupid fucker."

"Cartel guys normally have grenades?" Leo said.

Malone picked up the black bag with the cash and put one of the straps over his shoulder. "Anything's possible nowadays."

"Looks like Johnny's got the last one over there," Leo said. "Johnny's got him."

Malone and Leo walked toward the last Latin King and opened the bag on the ground, revealing the stacks of banded cash.

Malone moved his eyes from the bag to the man hand-cuffed in front of him. "Not bad. Tell me, how much is in there?"

Silence.

"See the rest of your crew over there on the ground?" Malone said. "You really wanna join 'em?"

The man stared back and said nothing.

"How much is it?"

"Fuck you, vato."

Malone walked over with his gun aimed at the man. "I'm getting sick of your bullshit. I said, how much money's in the bag?"

"Three hundred."

Malone kept the gun level with the man's head. "You're not bullshitting me, are you?"

"No—no. I ain't bullshitting ya."

"Good."

"Anything on this guy?" Malone said to Leo.

"He had a .38 on him."

"That it?"

"Yeah," Leo said.

"Want me to call this—" Johnny said.

Sudden gunfire rang out as Malone fired his P226 two times hitting the chest of the man in front of him. The man immediately tumbled down into the snow.

Johnny jumped. "What the hell was that? You just killed him in cold blood."

"Calm the fuck down," Malone said standing over the dead body. "Look in his hands. He had a grenade. One was on the driver too."

Johnny stepped closer and his eyes widened at the grenade.

"Fuck. I—I'm so sorry. He must have had it in his jacket or something. I shouldn't have..."

"It's okay. I don't blame you from where you were standing."

"Yeah," Johnny said with a sigh.

"It's over. You can relax. Here have a drink and call this in, okay?" Malone held out his flask.

Johnny nodded in agreement, took the flask, and went over to the car.

"Never a dull moment with you, is it?" Leo said.

"Tell me—did you see it in his hand?" Malone said.

"Nope. Glad you did or we'd all be floating around playing harps."

Malone stuffed his hands into his jacket as he looked at the four corpses on the ground. "We already got IAD up our ass. This ain't gonna help nothing."

"No, it's not," Leo said, "but nothing we can do about that."

"I gotta get rid of this gun."

"Wait, let's clear the warehouse and see if they have any video recordings."

"Good idea."

Malone and Leo hurried into the warehouse with guns drawn. The building was filled with boxes, pallets, and a forklift. In the corner was a small office. The door was open and inside was a desk, filing cabinets, an open laptop, and a card table with several beer bottles on top of it.

"Grab that," Malone said as he motioned toward the computer. "See if you can pull the hard drive."

"That'll take some time."

"We ain't got much of that."

Leo scrolled around using the trackpad and pecked on the keyboard to find any recordings from the cameras.

Malone paced in the office while he waited. He was tempted to get out his flask but then remembered he gave it to Johnny.

"Tell me you got something."

"No. There's nothing here. I've checked everything I can check. It's not here."

"Fucking shit!" Malone said as he slammed his fist into the side of the filing cabinet.

"Maybe those cameras outside are decoys?"

"You think?"

"There aren't any security video files on the computer."

"Okay, let's get the hell outta here."

Malone and Leo met Johnny by the door.

"Backup should be here in a few minutes."

"Okay," Malone said as he looked down at the bag of cash.

"Johnny, go get the dope. Bring it here."

Johnny picked up the bag and handed it over to Malone.

"This looks like about sixteen kilos," Malone said, "and that's supposed to be 300 grand in cash."

"Holy shit," Leo said.

"Yeah, this shit doesn't add up. If it's sixteen keys, that's worth a helluva lot more than that."

"Like a half a million," Leo said. "At least. Probably more."

Malone nodded. "Some of this shit's gotta disappear. Now. Otherwise, IAD is gonna think we took a bunch of cash."

"You're right," Leo agreed.

"You doing what I think you're doing?" Johnny said.

"We got no choice," Malone replied.

Malone took half of the sixteen blocks of heroin out of the bag and left it on the ground by Leo and Johnny.

"See if you can find another bag inside for the dope," Malone said to Leo.

"Sure thing."

Leo came back out and handed over a half-full trash bag.

"Only thing I could find."

"It'll work," Malone replied.

Malone could feel his heart beating faster as he moved the dope into the trash bag. Sweat beaded on his forehead. He listened for the sound of sirens but heard nothing. Then he heard Max's voice in his head.

"What the fuck are you doing man? Shit's good as cash. You're throwing your goddamn retirement into the river. Don't be stupid. Don't piss all that away."

Max's voice went away as Malone shook his head from side to side as he drove down the street. His eyes widened as he looked over at the trash bag in the passenger seat. He pulled over and tossed the trash bag off of the bridge watching it disappear in the dark water.

Malone returned to the warehouse to see Leo and Johnny standing in front of the U-Haul, the corpses scattered on the ground amongst the two bags filled with cash and drugs.

Malone walked over to Johnny and said, "Go get another drink. We're okay now. Really."

As Johnny walked to the car, Malone bent down and took out five stacks of cash and stuffed it under his shirt.

His eyes met Leo's and he nodded in agreement.

"How much was that?

"Fifty."

"Okay, good."

Johnny came back over.

Malone said, "Any better?"

"I will be."

Malone smiled.

"I've got some gum in the car. Lemme get you some."

"Thanks."

Malone pulled out the cash and put it into the glove box. Five wrapped stacks totaling fifty grand. He walked back to the warehouse as sirens blared in the distance.

"Here you go," Malone said as he handed Johnny a piece of gum.

"Appreciate it."

"Quite the evening, huh?" Leo said.

"Yeah, and it ain't even over yet," Malone replied.

Malone smoked his cigar by the U-Haul as backup arrived. An ambulance pulled up, and it made Malone nauseous as he thought of Max's bloody body being rolled out. He hunched over and vomited near the moving truck's tire.

"Shit," he mumbled aloud.

"You okay?" Leo asked.

Malone stood up and wiped his mouth with the back of his hand.

"Yeah, yeah. Just something I ate. I'm fine," Malone said, choking back the reflex to vomit again.

"You sure?"

"Yeah. I'm fine."

"I know what you're going through," Leo said. "He was my friend, too. Wanna talk about it?"

Malone yawned and looked up at the sky.

"Thanks, I'm fine. But I could use another drink."

"Me too. Soon as we fill out some paperwork, drinks are on me."

"Sounds like a plan."

CHAPTER TWELVE

Malone opened his eyes and saw the row of empty shot glasses in front of him on the bar. He fumbled out of his seat and walked awkwardly toward the small bathroom. As he stood at the urinal, he tried to recall what he did with the money from the U-Haul bust a few hours earlier. Then he remembered it was still in his car. Leo had said goodbye and left earlier during the night.

Malone slowly walked toward the bar and the bartender called his name. Malone mumbled, "I got a cab," and didn't look at the bartender as he went out the door.

His black Chevy Impala was covered with snow on the street. He got inside, quickly checked the glovebox for the cash, and saw the stacks were still there. He decided to move it and got out of the car. Using the sleeve of his jacket, he cleared some of the snow off of the trunk lid and looked around to see if anyone else was in sight. He waited for a car to pass, then opened the trunk, put the cash in a small grocery bag, and covered it with a blanket.

Relieved, he used the windshield wipers to clear the snow off and drove his car onto South State Street. He turned up the radio and sang along loudly to Guns N' Roses as his car started to slide on the snowy road. "Fucking snow!" he screamed as the car fishtailed on the white road. He drove in the middle of the road and jerked the wheel, causing the car to swerve to the side of the road. He skidded to a stop in a small snowbank. He put the car in reverse, pulled out of the snowbank, and was back on the road. After driving for a few minutes, he parked with one of the wheels up on the curb, staggered around to the trunk, and pulled the bag of cash out of his trunk.

As he opened the door to his apartment building, he looked back and realized he left the trunk open and went back and closed it. He entered his apartment, pulled the cash out of the bag, and laid it on the coffee table next to the couch. Malone then watched a Clint Eastwood movie until he fell asleep.

Malone woke to the roar of a snowblower outside. He slowly got up and made coffee, watching the stream of coffee sizzle as it landed into the pot. He heard his phone buzz across the room and hurried over to it. One missed call from Ann and another missed call from Johnny.

He took a shower to help him wake up and got dressed. He put a granola bar in his pocket, grabbed the bag of cash to deposit, and left his apartment. He tried calling Ann back, but the call went to voicemail.

Despite the usual fogginess from a hangover, Malone was in a surprisingly good mood. This new surge of cash would help the nest egg grow, not to mention a few less bad guys were on the streets.

He arrived at the storage unit, unlocked the door, and walked past all of the boxes. Each box full of memories of a different person living a different life. He walked over to the stack of plastic bins in the back and pulled the lid off of the blue plastic bin on the bottom. The bin was half full with banded stacks of cash in neat rows. Malone quickly filled the bin with the new cash. Malone put the lid on the top and pressed down hard to secure it in place.

"Guess I need to buy some more bins," Malone mumbled out loud.

Malone left the storage unit and saw a familiar Jeep parked next to his Chevy.

Johnny rolled down the window to the Jeep as Malone approached.

"Hey man," Johnny said. "Why didn't you call me back?"

"I was going to. Just stopping here first. You following me or something?"

"I had to. We gotta talk about what happened last night."

"Huh?"

"You wouldn't leave the bar. And you said you'd pull your gun on me if I made you leave."

"What the hell are you talking about?"

Malone watched Johnny's facial expression for a change, but it didn't. He was genuinely worried.

"I was joking, man. Blowing off some steam. Not too long ago I remember you were blowing off steam at your place, and I didn't give you any shit about it. Remember that?"

"Yeah," Johnny said.

"So then how 'bout you give me a fucking break?"

"You're right. Just wanted to make sure you were okay. You drank a lot last night. More than I've ever seen you have."

"You found me. Everything's fine. I'm going to headquarters. Come on, man. We good here?"

Johnny slowly nodded his head. "Yeah," he said. "Alright."

"I'll meet you at headquarters. Best to leave here separately."

"Yeah, you're right."

Malone watched Johnny drive down the street a couple of car lengths ahead of him. Malone's headache was getting worse and he really wanted a taste. He stopped at the corner and picked up a copy of the *Sun-Times*. He tossed the paper on the passenger seat, then pulled up to the liquor store where he bought two bottles of Jameson and left. Once in the car, he opened a bottle. After a few drinks, his headache started to fade.

Malone started the car and parked at a gas station across from St. Joseph's. He sat in the car drinking and noticed a blue Honda Odyssey pull into the parking lot. It was just like Ann's. His mind started moving slower as the liquor numbed his senses.

Ann was never the problem. The problem was the job. Hard to be a good husband or father when you're never home. And even when he was home, he wasn't really home. Malone wished he had a switch that he could flip on demand, but the closest thing he had was the drinking. Once a cop, always a cop. On duty, off duty, it didn't matter.

Malone knew he was swimming in the sludge and it wasn't fair to make her get dirty too. So he left before Ann had the chance to go herself. She was too Catholic to leave. But he knew she was only drowning with him. They barely talked, barely saw each other. Whenever they did, they were like two old friends passing each other on the street. After Malone moved out, Ann decided to get a real estate license. She spent more time with her friends. She had started moving on with her life as best she could.

Ann was a creature of habit. Judging from the time, she'd be picking up James from preschool about now. James would run out of preschool smiling and probably skipping on the sidewalk. Then they'd go home and have lunch together, talk about the day.

Malone took another drink from the bottle. He looked down at the bottle and put it back in the brown bag. He got out and went into the gas station and wandered down the aisles in a semi-buzzed haze. He bought coffee, some jerky, and chewing gum. As he walked back to the car, he pulled out his phone.

Ann picked up on the fourth ring.

"Hey, it's me," he said.

"Hi.

"Can I—uh—take James to get some ice cream or something? I'd love it if you could come too."

"I'm sorry but we can't. I gotta go to the grocery store and make lunch."

"Let me take you out for lunch?"

"Sorry, I've got a showing later this afternoon. I need to get groceries now."

"Where are you going?"

"The Whole Foods over on South Halstead."

"When?"

"Right now. Hopefully, he'll take a quick nap after lunch."

"Okay, I'll meet you over there in a few minutes."

"You're not working?"

"No, I took the day off."

"Oh—okay. Uh—yeah."

"See you in a few minutes," Malone said.

He saw Ann's blue van in the parking lot and parked a couple of spaces down from it. Ann was still in the car, and Malone waved at James in his car seat. She was thirty-four but looked like she was around twenty-five or so. She always looked good.

Malone walked over toward the van.

"Hi. How are you?"

"I'm fine. You?"

"Good."

The side door slid open and James was there, ready to jump out.

"Dad!" James said as he got out and ran toward Malone.

"Hey, buddy. Since when can you unbuckle yourself and get out of the car like that?"

"I put a sticker on my new truck. Wanna see it?

"Yeah. Show me."

"It's in my seat. Mom, can I bring it in?"

"Let's leave it in the car," Ann said.

"I'll check it out later," Malone said. "I promise."

"How was preschool today?"

"Good. I played with cars and we read a book about birds."

"Nice. You know, your mom likes robins." Malone smiled at Ann, who gave a slight smile back.

"I like Batman!" James replied.

Malone smiled. "Who doesn't?"

As they entered the store, Malone said, "Do you wanna sit in the cart?"

"Yeah. Can you push it?"

Malone set James in the cart and gently pushed it into the store.

"How are things going?" he asked Ann.

"Pretty good. Starting to get some showings."

"I'm sure you'll do great." He looked at James. "He's getting taller and taller."

"Yeah, sure is. Just like a weed. Can't keep him in clothes that fit."

"I bet. Do you need some money for clothes?"

"That'd help a lot, yeah."

Malone pulled out his wallet and gave Ann a couple of twenties.

"Sorry, that's all I have on me."

"No, that helps."

"Good."

Ann got closer to Malone and spoke in a near whisper. "First time you've seen him for more than thirty seconds in what, a month?"

"I've been busy. You know with Max and everything."

"Yeah, I know. It's always something." Ann turned her head away and looked at apples on a brown wooden crate. When her phone rang, she pulled it out of her purse and answered it. "Hey, Josh. I'm good. How are you?" She covered her phone with her hand. "I've got to take this, can you two get some bread, milk, and jelly?"

Malone nodded and kept pushing the cart down the aisle.

"How was the zoo the other day?"

"Good. I saw bears, lions, tigers, and zebras."

"That's great. Do you like grape or strawberry jelly?"

"Grape!"

"Alright, grape it is." Malone placed the jar in the cart.

Malone saw Ann walk toward them.

"There you are," she said.

"Here we are. Who's this Josh guy?"

"He's a client. I've got a showing with him later today. He just wanted to confirm the location. He wasn't sure where it was exactly."

"If you say so."

"Yeah, that's all. Wait a second—" Ann stepped closer and lowered her voice. "I can smell that booze on your breath. You're gonna kill yourself or someone else. You know that?"

"Look, I can explain." Malone raised a hand up as if each word he said carried some weight.

"I don't wanna hear some BS story. Sometime when you're actually sober—if that ever happens—you can see your son. But right now, you need to leave."

"Wait. Wait, let me explain," Malone said.

"No. Go. Go now. Just go."

Malone stopped pushing the cart and looked at Ann's deep blue eyes.

"Alright. I'm sorry, okay? I'm really sorry." He turned to James. "Hey, pal. I gotta go. I gotta go catch one of the bad guys. Next time I see you I'm gonna bring you something fun, okay? Can I get a hug?"

Malone started to walk around to the front of the cart toward James, but Ann stepped in front of Malone, blocking him from hugging James.

"No. Not when you've been drinking."

Malone slowly nodded his head and opened his mouth, but the words wouldn't come out. "I'll—uh—see you, pal. I—gotta go. Love you."

Malone stuffed his hands into the pockets of his jeans and looked down at the ground as if following a string that led back to his car. Once he got into the driver's seat, he pulled the flask out of the glovebox and held it in his hand. He unscrewed the lid and just held it in his hand a few inches from his lips. He moved it away, put the lid back on, and shoved it into the glovebox. He pulled out his phone and called Leo.

"Hey, it's me. You down at the station?"

"Yeah," Leo said.

"Johnny there?"

"Just called, said he was doing some errands."

"Okay. I'll be there in a few minutes. I'm on my way."

"Alright, see you in a few."

Malone shifted the car into drive, but something inside wouldn't let him leave. Not yet. He pulled into another empty space on the other side of the parking lot and sat in silence. Malone saw Ann and James come out of the store and walk out into the snowy parking lot. She brushed a strand of hair out of her face revealing her furrowed brow. She had the same expression on her face when she first left the hospital after James was born. Malone closed his eyes. So much had changed over the years, but at the same time, so much was still the same.

CHAPTER THIRTEEN

Malone pulled up to headquarters and popped a piece of gum in his mouth. Once inside, he saw that Leo was at his desk staring at the computer. Malone walked toward him and stopped next to his desk.

"Hey. How you feeling?"

"A little under the weather. I can't keep up with you."

"That's probably a good thing."

Leo laughed. "Yeah. How are you?"

"Same as you. I'll be okay. Find out anything about the buyers or sellers?"

"Nothing yet."

"An entire shipment and the cash disappearing is bound to stir things up. Could even start a gang war if the Kings think another gang had something to do with it."

"Agreed."

"What about the moving truck?"

"I ran the plates. It's from a used car dealer in Milwaukee."

"Nice. Not too far either."

"Is a road trip in order?"

"Yeah, I think so."

Johnny walked into the GTF office with a mug in his hand.

"Hey, guys."

"Where were you?"

"Had to run a couple errands. I'll make the time up."

"Shit. Don't worry about it."

"The U-Haul was from Milwaukee," Malone said to Johnny as his eyes looked at the computer screen. "Says here they're open until 6."

"Time for a road trip?"

"You read my mind," Malone said to Johnny. He turned to Leo. "Why don't you stay here in case something comes up."

Leo nodded.

Johnny took a drink of coffee and set the mug down on the desk.

"When you wanna leave?"

"How about we roll out now? We'll beat some traffic."

"Okay, sure."

Johnny followed Malone out to his car, sat down in the passenger seat, pulled a red Marlboro wrapper out of the seat, and held it up.

"I thought you only smoked cigars?"

"Max was always leaving shit in here," Malone said, his voice trailing off.

"How long was he your partner?"

"About two and a half years," Malone said with a yawn. "Let's listen to the radio for a while, huh?"

"Yeah, sure."

Malone was glad to get out of Chicago for a few hours. The change of scenery would be nice. He only wished he could make a whole day of it.

"Do we need to check in with anyone before we go out of town?"

"Hell no. We're pursuing a lead, not going to a Brewers game."

Johnny didn't reply.

"Where'd you go this morning, before you came to the office?" Malone said.

"Finding a gift for my girlfriend. It's our anniversary tonight. Thinking about proposing sometime soon."

"Need more on your plate do ya?" Malone said with a chuckle.

"I don't know. I guess. You married?"

"Separated. I moved out about six months ago. Married twelve years before that."

"That hard being a cop in a relationship?"

"You could say that." Malone noticed that Johnny looked uncomfortable and sweaty. "You feeling okay? Kinda look like shit."

"Think I'm coming down with a cold."

"Drink some green tea. It really helps."

"Think that's the first time I've heard you say to drink something that doesn't involve alcohol."

"Well, some whiskey wouldn't hurt either."

"There it is," Johnny said as both men laughed.

"You a Bulls fan?" Malone said.

"Yeah, I watch a few games."

"Buddy of mine said the Lakers were at Prysm until 3 in the morning. We could put something down on them."

"Thanks, but all of my cash is tied up on that ring. No gambling for me. I don't have a good history with gambling anyways. It's not for me."

Malone nodded.

"I know you're younger, but did you ever hear stories about when Jordan would go out all night in Atlantic City and still score at will on the Knicks? I remember one game he scored 54 points. Probably haunts Knicks fans to this day."

"I've heard the stories. Seen some of the highlights."

"I've never seen anything like it before. When you can't beat someone no matter what—it grates on the nerves. Like fighting something so big you can't even understand it."

"I bet. We talking about Jordan or the job?"

"A lot in common there, huh."

Malone's phone rang and he picked up.

"Yeah, Malone."

"It's Carver. I need you for a news conference the Chief and Mayor are holding later today."

"You shitting me?"

"Nope. Just heard about it myself. Down at City Hall."

"Look—I can't make it. I'm following up on a lead."

"This ain't a request, Malone. Like I said, it's the Mayor and the Chief. Requested your crazy ass by name."

Malone sighed. "Shit. Let me guess, all of us standing together by the dope on the table, right?"

"You know it. And my ass'll be right there standing next to yours."

"Sure you can't get me out of this? I'm on my way to fucking Milwaukee following a lead on that case."

"You gotta take the wins, Malone. This is a win, dammit. Get your ass down there, you hear me?"

"Yes, sir," Malone said, trying to hold in his anger.

"I know that meant 'fuck you,' Malone. You're not as smart as you think you are."

Malone hung up and slapped his hands down on the steering wheel. "Bunch of motherfucking shit!" he yelled.

"Problem?"

"News conference in about an hour. Want me to stand there with all the suits next to the dope on the table. Bunch of bullshit."

"You have a suit? I've never seen you in one."

"Yeah, I own a goddamn suit. I just don't wear it much."

"Oh, okay."

"Do I own a suit? What kinda question is that?" Malone said as he flipped on the siren and did a u-turn on I-41, cutting over to the other side of the interstate.

"We'll hit Milwaukee later," he said as he pressed down on the accelerator and passed a green mile marker sign, speeding back toward Chicago.

CHAPTER FOURTEEN

Malone straightened his tie as he entered the crowded conference room. Photographers and journalists were crammed on top of each other. Malone did not look directly at them. He stood next to Carver, his face blank as he waited for the press conference to start.

Mayor Wallace came out. The press stood up and took pictures as he shook hands with Police Chief Myers. Wallace then stood behind the podium and started his speech.

Malone's eyes drifted toward Myers, who slightly nodded in his direction. Malone nodded back and shifted his eyes to the stacks of heroin and cash on the table. It wasn't until the mayor started to ramble that Malone shifted his eyes straight ahead toward the crowd directly in front of him. He then saw Johnny and Leo lined up in the front next to a few other officers in uniform and flashed a half a smile and then bounced his eyes again to the back of the room.

Wallace then invited Myers to speak and he made some final remarks.

Malone heard Carver's name said aloud and then heard his name mentioned. He instinctively nodded again at Myers and mouthed "Thank you," and stood silently again. The press asked some questions but the mayor's assistant replied, "No questions at this time. Thank you all for coming."

Myers and Wallace filed out of the room and Malone moved ahead toward Johnny, Leo, and the other officers.

"Looking good up there, Malone," said one of the officers in uniform.

"Yeah, yeah. Go fuck yourself."

"A job well done," Leo said.

"You deserve credit, too. We're a team, so wipe that shit-eating grin off your face, will ya?" Malone said to Johnny. "Let's get the hell out of here."

The three left headquarters and strolled into the parking lot.

"How bout you drive?" Malone said as he gave the keys to Johnny.

"Uh, yeah, sure."

Malone looked over at Leo who had wide eyes.

"What?"

"You—uh—normally don't let someone else drive unless you're already loaded. Even then I've never seen you willingly hand over the keys. You been hitting it early today?"

"No, I'm just fucking tired of driving," Malone said. "But if you're gonna be a prick about it, I'll drive."

"I see," Leo said as he stared back at Malone. Johnny gave the keys back.

"I did have a small taste to calm my nerves before going into the shit show," Malone said.

"You're not worried that someone might smell it on you?"

"Cigars and gum cover that shit up."

"Sure."

"How bout we take our little road trip instead of jerking each other off here in the parking lot?"

"I—uhh," Johnny said.

"Come on player," Malone interrupted, "I know you got a hot date tonight," Malone said as he looked at his watch. "It's what—uh—three now. You'll be back by six, loverboy."

"You sure?" Johnny said, "Reservations at Monteverde were hard to come by."

"Yeah. Absolutely."

Malone turned to Leo. "You wanna tag along?"

"Thanks, but I think I'll just keep looking around to see what I can find if that's alright with you."

"Yeah, sure. But you're gonna miss all the fun."

"If you say so. I'll call you if I find out anything."

CHAPTER FIFTEEN

Johnny climbed into Malone's car and buckled his seatbelt. "Do you have a plan for how you want to approach this guy?"

"Just roll with it and feel him out. A huge part of the job is just reading people."

"Okay. You're thinking we'll be back by six?"

"Oh yeah, no problem. What time is your reservation again?"

"Seven o'clock."

"Okay then. Let's get our asses to Milwaukee." Malone pressed down on the accelerator and started passing the other cars on the expressway.

"Thanks."

"No problem. You need something, ask. We gotta look out for each other."

The two drove in silence until Malone pulled into a used car lot with three U-haul trucks parked to the side of a small building.

"Look at that, right at an hour," Malone said.

"That's pretty good."

"Pretty good? That's damn good. Just saved us thirty minutes, easy."

Johnny followed Malone into the rectangular office. An older man was talking on the phone behind a desk. He wore glasses too small for his face framed by thin, black hair. He had a white, polo shirt embroidered with a small company logo. He held up his hand and half waved at Malone.

"Look I gotta go," he said into the phone. "I know. I know. Yeah, yeah. I'll pick it up on the way home."

He hung up and stepped around his desk.

"Hi there, welcome to Marty's Used Car Lot. I'm Marty. Ready to find the perfect car at a great price?"

Malone held up his badge. "Actually, we just need some information."

"Uh—what's the problem, officer?" Marty said as he sat down, partially leaning on the corner of his desk for a moment before moving back to his chair.

"Can we sit down?" Johnny said.

"Oh yeah. Please, take a seat."

Malone and Johnny sat down in the two chairs that faced Marty's desk.

"Did you recently rent a U-Haul to someone driving into Chicago?"

"Well, we rent quite a few vehicles. I have different ones coming and going all the time. Including drop-offs from out of state."

"We need everything you've got on this truck right here," Johnny said, holding out a photo of a license plate.

Marty took it from Johnny and looked down.

"The individual who rented this truck was involved in a crime in Chicago," Johnny said. "I need a name, address, whatever info he gave you."

"I'm confused. A crime? What crime?"

Malone glanced over at Johnny and then scanned the

office, looking at the several plaques on the wall, the dated, black and white photos, and the framed dollar bill.

"Got a bathroom?" Malone said.

"Yes. It's straight back and on the right."

Malone got up and found the restroom which consisted of a toilet and a sink in a small, dimly lit room. He relieved himself and washed his hands. As he closed the door, he heard Johnny's voice.

"You can comply, or we can get the FBI involved. This issue crosses state lines, so the FBI would have jurisdiction."

Malone sat back down as Marty spoke. "I—I don't want any trouble," he said.

Marty rose out of his chair and opened the grey filing cabinet behind his desk. Marty thumbed through the files as Malone looked out at the cars for sale on the lot. Ten used cars, all several years old. Malone knew Marty couldn't be making a good living from the car and moving truck rentals alone.

"How's it going over there?" Malone said.

"Here it is," Marty said as he pulled out a file folder. "It—uh—looks like it is for Manuel Rodriguez."

Malone took the document, glanced it over, and handed it back.

"Make a copy?"

"Yes, of course."

Marty took the paperwork and set it on the copier.

"I assume you want a copy of the full contract as well?"

"Yeah, that's perfect. Do you run any credit reports or background checks?"

"A copy of a valid driver's license is all that is required." Marty looked down at the contract. "This specific customer paid in cash, so he had to pay the entire fee upfront plus the two hundred fifty dollar deposit."

"Has this individual rented from you before?"

Marty sat back down and the keys clattered on his keyboard as he typed. "Just one minute—yes. It looks like he did rent a fifteen-footer on August 21st."

"Can you pull that receipt too?"

"Yeah—uhh—I think it's uhh..." Marty muttered as he went back to the filing cabinet and flicked through the file folders. "Here it is."

He turned and set the paperwork on the copy machine and pressed the button before Malone could tell him to make a copy.

"Here you go," Marty said as he held out the pages.

Malone handed the contract to Johnny and turned back to Marty.

"Thanks for all of your help. Really appreciate it. What can you tell me about that F-150 out there?"

"Would love to show it to you."

"Sure, yeah. Quite a looker."

"Couldn't agree more."

Malone and Marty went out in the lot and walked past several SUVs and sedans and stopped at a dark red Ford F150.

"Just got this in last week. The previous owner gets a new model every two years like clockwork. It's practically new."

Malone strolled around the truck and opened the driver's door.

"Wow, it's really clean," he said.

"Yeah, she's a beaut. Previous owner babied her. Never even took her out in the snow. Would you like to take it for a test drive?"

"I'll think about it."

"Sure. Just know it'll likely be gone if you wait too long."

Marty handed Malone a white business card with the picture of a car on it.

"Thanks," Malone said as he glanced down at the card.

Malone and Johnny walked back to the black sedan and got in.

Johnny turned to Malone. "Didn't know you liked trucks."

"I don't give a shit about trucks," Malone said.

"Just going after his cell number, huh?"

"And getting on his good graces. See how quickly he changed his tune when I mentioned the truck?"

"Yeah. It was like a switch flipped or something."

"Umm-hmm."

"You thinking he's dirty?"

"Not sure. Could just be another car salesman, right?"

Malone rubbed his eye as he drove down the road. "Tell me something. Was that truck supposed to be returned to the same location?"

Johnny flipped through the contract and scanned the pages quickly. "No, looks like it was going to be dropped off in Chicago. The West Cermak location."

"When?" Malone glanced over at Johnny.

Johnny flipped through the stack of paper in his hands.

"Yeah, looks like it was scheduled to be dropped off yesterday."

"Say someone threatened Marty. He'd do whatever they want and sit there worrying in his little office giving himself an ulcer."

"Yeah, he would."

"Perfect patsy. Lemme know if you see anything else on those contracts."

Malone turned up the radio slightly and yawned again while Johnny read the documents.

A few minutes later, Johnny spoke. "Looks like this Rodriguez used a different address each time he rented a truck. An apartment in California. His driver's license says California too, but doesn't match either address he has listed."

"Anything in common?"

"San Diego."

"Shit, that might as well be fucking Mexico. That means the cartel is using the same mules. When you're moving millions of dollars worth of smack, you gotta be pretty cautious."

"You thinking the cartel has Marty under surveillance?"

"Absolutely. Sounds like I wanna go for a test drive after all."

Malone turned the car around causing the car to fishtail slightly as he drove back to the car lot.

Malone opened the door to the office causing Marty to look up from the paperwork on the desk.

"You change your mind on that F-150?"

"Yeah. Let's go for a test drive," Malone replied.

"Alrighty—you wanna meet me out there? I'll grab the keys."

"Yeah, sure."

Malone stepped out of the office and met Johnny outside.

"Any plans here you want to tell me about?"

"Haven't you noticed that I like to wing it by now?"

"C'mon, Malone. You got something in mind."

"Make sure your seat belt is buckled."

"Shit, I think I'll just stay right here."

"Suit yourself."

"Okay," Marty said, holding out the keys to Malone. "Let's go for a ride in this beauty."

"Be back in a few minutes," Malone said with a smile to Johnny.

Malone sat behind the wheel and Marty climbed into the passenger seat.

He turned the key in the ignition and pulled out onto the road, pressing down on the accelerator. Marty held on to the handgrip above the window.

"She's got some power, huh," Marty said.

"Damn right," Malone said as he pressed down harder on the gas pedal and smiled back at Marty.

"How about you cut the shit now. Tell me what the fuck is going on."

"Excuse me? What—do you mean? What are you talking about?"

"Don't know what I'm talking about, huh?" Malone pressed the pedal down further. "Cut the shit, or I'm gonna test the brakes here. You're gonna watch your lunch go all over the dashboard. We might even test out the airbags."

"I—t—told you. I don't know what you want," Marty said.

"Okay, here we go."

Malone slammed down hard on the brakes and Marty's body jerked forward and nearly hit the dashboard.

"These brakes really are solid, aren't they? Look, just tell me what you know. I'm sure they threatened you, said they were gonna hurt your family. You're not in trouble. I ain't after you. I'm after them."

Marty coughed again and Malone jammed his foot back on the accelerator.

"Really wanna test the brakes again?" Malone asked.

"What—what are you talking about?" Marty said.

Malone pulled the truck off to the side of the road and walked around to the passenger door, yanking Marty from the vehicle.

"I'm getting sick of the bullshit."

"Wait, what are you talking about?"

"Look—the fucking cartel is using your trucks to move drugs," Malone said as he exhaled.

"Cartel? No, no, no. The truck rental was just like all the others. Nothing unusual at all. Nothing."

"The last truck was filled with heroin."

"What? They're drug dealers? I—I can't believe this. You think they are watching me? My phone, my internet?"

"There's a damn good chance."

"Oh god—oh god," Marty said as he held his hand on his chest.

"You okay?" Malone said.

"I—have asthma. Need—inhaler."

Malone helped Marty back into the vehicle and flew down the road. Soon they were back at the dealership. Malone jumped out of the truck with Marty coughing and gasping for air.

"What the hell?" Johnny said.

"He's got asthma," Malone said as he helped Marty inside.

Marty pulled the inhaler from his desk and used it to take a deep breath. Soon he started breathing better.

"You good now?" Johnny said.

"Yeah. Yeah," Marty said and followed his words with a cough. "I think so."

"Anyone been out here repairing anything in the last few months? Utilities, phone, anything."

Marty shook his head.

Malone walked over to Marty's desk. "Step back," he said.

"What are you doing?"

"You heard me—move."

Marty got out of his chair and Malone searched the computer and desk for bugs.

"What're you doing? I don't know anything."

Malone stood back up and got in Marty's face. "Think about it for a minute. Anything at all. They didn't threaten you or give you any hush money or anything?"

Johnny searched the electrical outlets and light fixtures

for bugs while Malone checked the furniture and picture frames.

"How did the customer contact you last time?"

"He called me one day in advance and asked if I had any trucks ready. That's it—really."

"You're sure?

"Yeah. That's it."

"Nothing strange at all?" Johnny said.

"No—nope. He paid in cash. But that's not too uncommon."

"Okay, fine—but you need to be careful. Don't tell your wife about this or anyone else. You see anything at all even remotely out of the ordinary, here's my number. Call me immediately."

Malone wrote down his number on a piece of paper and handed it to him.

"Okay—I will."

Malone and Johnny left the building and got back in the car.

"You know he's probably gonna have a heart attack now, right?"

"Yeah, maybe. But at least he'll be alert now. And he won't hesitate to call if anything seems out of the ordinary. Why don't you check in with Leo and let him know what we found?"

"Yeah. Sure." Malone felt some adrenaline building in his gut as he heard Johnny recite the information out loud. The case was coming together, one piece at a time. It was starting to make sense.

Johnny hung up. "Alright, Leo's gonna dig into this, run an INTERPOL on Rodriguez and see what pops up."

"Good. No gang wars at the moment?" Malone asked with a cigar in his mouth.

"Nothing more than normal."

"I guess that's good news."

"You know with this going back to California, we're probably looking at a Federal matter."

"Yeah. Feds with agendas. Fuck 'em. I'm just focusing on how this shit flows downstream to Chicago."

"You ever follow any rules?"

"Every now and then. Besides, I got you and Leo to help keep me on the straight and narrow."

Johnny grinned.

"We just gotta keep taking 'em down, one piece at a time. This shit is building to something bigger."

"Yeah, sure seems like it."

Malone and Johnny drove the rest of the way back to Chicago in silence.

CHAPTER SIXTEEN

Malone parked by the station. "Look at that," he said to Johnny. "You've still got over an hour before your date."

"Yeah, that's pretty good," Johnny said as he got out of the car.

Malone rolled down the window. "Hey," he called.

Johnny turned around.

"Have a good night, Romeo. See you in the morning."

Johnny smiled. "Good night."

Malone turned off the car and went inside to find Leo sitting down at his desk writing on a legal pad.

"Here are the documents for the truck," Malone said, handing the paperwork to Leo.

"Okay, good. Thanks."

"Think this is the first time I've walked in here and not seen you staring at the computer. Working on this week's grocery list?"

"Very funny. I do some of my best thinking not staring at a screen."

"Someone told me I do my best thinking at the bar," Malone said with a half-smile.

"Sounds like something Max would say," Leo said as he flipped through the documents.

"Yeah," Malone said. "It was…"

"This trail might be too clean," Leo said. "This is really straightforward. I'd expect more from the cartel."

"Maybe the cartel hired a runner that es no bueno."

"Yeah. Maybe." Leo kept looking at the documents.

"You said this could be New Gens, right?" Malone asked. "A spinoff from the Sinaloa?"

"Yeah, that's what I'm thinking."

"Say you're right. If you're smaller, you have less options, right? Maybe they're doing that. Just using more fear tactics. Scare the shit out of us."

"Yeah. Most likely."

"I did find this from the Feds," Malone pointed to his computer. Leo hunched over, looking at the screen. "A few years ago, the New Gens dismembered the remains of fourteen men. They stuffed the remains in plastic bags and put them in the back of a minivan. They wanted to send a message to Los Zetas."

"That's quite the message," Leo said.

"If you pull off that kind of shit, you're not too worried about covering your tracks, right?"

"Yeah, I agree. How'd it go with Johnny?"

"Pretty good. He held his own."

"Oh really? That's good."

"You sound surprised."

"A little bit, yeah."

"He's young. Just needs more practice in the field. He'll get better."

"Yeah, that would help for sure."

"You staying much longer?"

"Just going over these documents for a few more minutes. Then I'm heading home."

"Okay, don't stay too late. Get some rest."

"Yeah, good night."

"See you in the morning," Malone said through a yawn as left the office.

Malone stopped at a diner where he ate a club sandwich with black coffee. He tried calling Ann, but the call went directly to voicemail.

As he walked down the street, Malone realized that he was treading the fine line between wired and exhausted. He couldn't decide if he wanted to go to sleep or to the gym to work out. He yawned again and decided that sleep would do him some good.

He drove to his apartment and stopped at the door. He pulled out his phone and tried calling Ann again and this time left a voicemail. "Hey. I screwed up. I was hoping we could talk. I'll see you. Bye."

Malone put his key into the apartment door and opened it. As he stepped inside, he dropped his keys on the floor, the clattering sound echoing through the apartment. As he bent down to pick them up, a blast rang out from the other side of the apartment.

A shotgun. The sound of the blast left Malone stunned and disoriented. He stayed on the ground, drew his P226, and fired a burst in the general direction of the shooter. He waited for more return fire, but nothing came. He stayed down, watching for any sign of movement in the dark. Nothing.

Malone slowly crawled on his hands and knees toward the other side of the apartment with a window. As he inched closer, he crouched and saw a shadow move in the moonlight. Malone picked up a half-empty beer bottle and tossed it across the room hitting the wall. The gunman appeared in sight and Malone ducked back behind a chair as another boom from the shotgun filled the room, this time blasting the TV to pieces.

Malone fired again at the gunman, the first shot hitting him in the shoulder, spinning him to the right and the second hit him on the other side. Malone fired again, hitting the gunman in the head. Blood splattered the off-white wall. The gunman fell to the floor and Malone slowly approached, keeping his gun aimed at him.

Malone pulled a flashlight from a drawer and got a better look at the gunman. A young Latino, his eyes now dull and lifeless. Malone felt his pockets. Nothing. He lifted his shirt. No ink on his chest or arms. Didn't look like he was a Latin King or anyone he knew with local ties.

"Motherfucking shit," he said under his breath.

Malone took a deep breath as another thought crossed his mind: what if he'd been greenlit by a cartel?

Malone tried calling Ann on his cell but the call went to voicemail. He tried to think clearly, but instinct had completely taken over.

On the road, he tried calling Leo as he swerved around a yellow cab on South Halstead.

"Leo?"

"Yeah."

"Some asshole just tried to take me out in my apartment with a shotgun—might've been from a cartel."

"Shit! You okay?"

"Yeah, close fucking call, but I'm okay. We gotta let Johnny know and make sure he's safe. I'm going to Ann's now."

"Will do. Anything else?"

"Send a squad over to Ann's. And my place. Watch your ass. If I'm greenlit, the whole team could be too."

Malone hung up, his hands shaking from adrenaline. He dialed Ann's number again. Voicemail. Fuck.

Malone felt a sinking feeling in his gut. He hoped she was still just pissed off at him. He sped up and weaved in and out of traffic. "Move it, asshole!" Malone barked as he swerved around a businessman in a Mercedes sedan who honked his horn and threw up a middle finger.

Malone flipped on his siren. He took a wide left turn and his headlight tore off the side mirror on a pickup truck. He kept going until he hit a construction zone that led down 73rd St. Malone drove around the construction barrels and swerved out to the sound of honking horns. A semi barreled down the street head-on toward Malone.

"Fucking move it!" Malone screamed.

The semi pulled off to the side at the last second. He growled in anger and frustration. He tried calling Ann again. Voicemail.

"Motherfucker!"

Once he hung up, Leo called.

"Yeah?"

"I sent a squad over to Ann's. I'm gonna pass you through to them. Should just take a second."

Malone waited and then heard a voice on the line.

"Sargent Malone, this is Officer Al Lopez. The residence is fine. Looks secure. Nothing going on over here."

"You sure?"

"Yes. The doors are locked, all the lights are out. No signs of any disturbance."

"Did you get ahold of anyone?"

"No, I don't think anyone is home."

"Okay, can you stay there? I'm just a few minutes out."

"Yeah, sure."

"Thanks."

Malone wanted to believe everything was fine, but his

mind was flooded with gruesome scenarios and horrific sights. Images flashing inside his head about the cartel and the bodies in the van. He shook his head to erase the images and pressed down harder on the gas pedal, the engine roaring as he flew down the road.

As he turned down Ann's street, he skidded to a stop in front of her house. He jumped out of the car and met the officer in the cruiser.

"Like I said on the radio," Lopez said, "it looks like no one's home."

"Okay, thanks for stopping by."

The officer waved back as he drove away. Malone followed the sidewalk to the door. He rang the doorbell and waited a few moments, but no one came.

"Come on, Ann. Where the fuck are you?" he said aloud.

As he waited by the door, he had a bitter taste in his mouth and leaned over and spit in the bushes. Then Malone coughed a couple of times, and tried to ignore the feeling. He unholstered his P226, unlocked the door with his old house key, and entered through the kitchen. His eyes darted to each corner, each doorway, anywhere that would be a good place for an ambush. He searched each room for Ann and James. He heard a noise off to the left of the living room and rushed into the room.

"Freeze, motherfucker!" he blurted out, then stopped suddenly as he saw an orange cat staring back at him. Malone took a deep breath and ran up the stairs.

"Ann?" he called. "Ann? You there? Ann?" His voice got louder with each step. He opened the bedroom door. The bed was made. The bathroom door was shut and he could see light coming through the edge of the door. Malone slowly opened it. "Ann?"

Ann was in the bathtub with her eyes closed.

"Ann? Ann?"

As he got closer, he saw a small cord leading to head-phones in her ears.

Ann jerked her head and screamed. "Ryan?! You just scared the shit out of me. What the hell are you doing?"

"Wanted to make sure you're alright."

"What the hell is wrong with you?" Ann crossed her arms to cover herself while in the tub. "Let me guess, you were drinking and got lonely so you decided to come over here. Tell me I'm wrong."

"No, no. Get out of there. Get dressed, now."

"What the fuck, Ryan? You're not making any sense. You're really shit-faced, aren't you?"

"Look," he said. "You're not safe here. A few minutes ago someone ambushed me in my apartment."

"What? Are you serious?" Ann got out of the tub and wrapped a white towel around herself.

"Yeah. He was waiting for me at my place. If I hadn't dropped my keys, you'd be identifying pieces of me at the morgue."

Ann's eyes widened. "Shit. Are you okay?"

"I'm alright. Just wanted to be sure you guys are safe."

"I'm fine. James—"

Malone hurried toward his son's bedroom and saw him sound asleep in his bed. After letting out a sigh of relief, he turned back to see Ann in a towel in the doorway.

"He's asleep in bed," he said. "He's fine."

Ann let out a deep breath and walked back to the bath-room as Malone followed her. "Are we okay here?" she asked.

"There are some cruisers nearby, keeping an eye on the place. We should be fine."

"Okay."

"Didn't mean to scare you," Malone said. "I'll give you some privacy." He looked at the empty walls and remembered how they were once filled with family photos.

He entered James' room and kissed him on the forehead. He stood there for a moment, just watching his son sleep. He somehow looked older since the last time he saw him at the grocery store.

A loud sound rang out as the window across the room shattered. More loud sounds. Malone jumped on top of James, covering him with his body.

"Ann!" he screamed. "Ann! Get down!"

He held James tight as his son's screams mixed with the sound of gunfire slamming against the house.

After a few seconds, the gunfire stopped. Malone looked down at James. "You okay, buddy? Sorry to scare you."

James was crying and shaking, still covering his ears. "Arrgghh! Make it stop! Make it stop!"

"It's over, pal. You're safe now. You're safe."

Malone held his hands over James' ears. "Ann?" he screamed. "Ann?"

No response. He looked down at James and picked him up.

"Let's go find Mom."

Malone slowly walked into the hallway as a million fucked up scenarios flooded his mind.

He then saw Ann on the floor, curled into a ball, crying.

"You okay?" Malone said as he sat down with James in his arms. "You hit?"

"I'm—I'm—okay."

Ann reached over and Malone put James in her arms.

"He's okay," Malone said. "He's okay."

Ann looked up at Malone, her face pale and eyes bloodshot. Malone realized she had blood on her hand.

"There's some blood on your hand. Sure you're okay?"

She nodded slowly.

"Let me take a look at it." He knelt down.

"I'm fine," Ann said in a quiet voice. "Just a scratch on my leg from some of the broken glass."

"I hear you. Just let me take a quick look."

She flinched.

"Yeah, that glass got you pretty good. I'll go get something to help with that." Malone found the bandages in the bathroom. He carefully cleaned the wounds on her leg and bandaged them.

Malone then called in to report what happened. He quickly called Leo.

Within a few minutes, Lopez and his partner, Davis, were at the door. Malone filled them in and showed them James' room and the broken glass inside the house. After a few hours of paperwork and gathering evidence, Malone was done talking to them. As the officers left, Malone walked back around the outside of the house, looking at the damage - the bullet holes in the window of his son's bedroom. Malone went back inside and put a piece of cardboard over the window. He then found James and Ann both sound asleep downstairs. Malone paused and watched them sleep. He covered James with a blanket and kissed his forehead.

Ann woke up and their eyes met.

"Come here. There's plenty of room," Ann said as she held out her arms to Malone. He laid down next to Ann and she wrapped her arms around him and he closed his eyes.

CHAPTER SEVENTEEN

Malone jerked his head up as he woke to the sound of sirens outside. A loud knocking on the front door. He pulled his gun out of the holster and pointed his gun at the door. He looked back to Ann.

"Go upstairs," he said. "Tell me what kind of car is out front."

Ann nodded and quickly left the room.

Another loud knock on the door.

James woke up and started to cry.

"It's okay pal," Malone said. "I'll be right there, I promise." He kept his eyes and gun on the door, holding his breath as he waited for Ann's voice.

Ann stepped into the hallway. "It's a police cruiser," she said.

"Okay, good."

He took a deep breath, then loudly said, "Who is it?" as he stepped away from James, carefully walking toward the door.

"Hey, Malone. It's Lopez. Got Davis here too. We need to talk to you again."

Malone saw the two men in uniform through the peep-hole and slowly opened the door with this left hand and kept the P226 in his right hand behind his back. He turned around and looked at Ann and James

"It's okay," he said. "I'll be right back. Just be a minute."

Ann nodded her head slowly. James was still quietly crying.

Malone stepped out of the house and stood on the porch.

"Got some info for you," Lopez said.

"Oh?"

"Earlier tonight a neighbor reported seeing a black SUV pull up, fire at your residence, and leave," Lopez said. "And we just found an SUV matching that description—a Ford Explorer—abandoned a few miles from here. It was set on fire."

"Anything left of it?"

"Not much. Pretty sure it was stolen too."

"Shit," Malone said. "Just another day in Chicago."

"You been on the Gang Task Force for a while, right?" Davis said.

"Yeah, about four years. A non-stop shit show. Guess we've got some job security, huh?"

Davis and Lopez laughed.

"Who'd you talk to in Fire about the car?"

"Can't remember," Lopez said.

"But if you wanna see what's left of it, you better get over there now," Davis said. "It's by Donovan Park on West 37th."

"Okay, thanks. Let me know if you find out anything else."

"Yeah, sure," Lopez said before he left.

Malone went back inside. Ann held James in her arms on the couch. He leaned over and kissed James on the forehead and put his arm around Ann.

"You okay?" Malone said.

"No, I'm not."

"Fair enough. Why don't you try to get some more rest."

"Yeah—you're—right," Ann replied with a yawn in between her words.

"I'll be right back, just want to get something from upstairs."

He pulled out his phone when he got upstairs.

"Hey. I need some help."

"What can I do?" Leo said.

"They found the vehicle the shooters used. Torched it. I need you to go check it out."

"Where is it?"

"West 37th by Donovan Park."

"Okay, I'll let you know if I find anything."

"Thanks."

After Malone hung up, he picked a green stuffed dinosaur off the floor and carried it downstairs, then carefully tucked it under his son's arm. Malone laid down next to Ann on the couch and slowly fell asleep as he listened to the sound of his son breathing.

The next morning, Malone woke up to the sound of his cell phone ringing. Malone saw Ann and James asleep in a chair on the other side of the room. Malone picked up the phone.

"Where the hell are you?" the caller asked.

Malone rubbed his eyes and tried to place the voice.

"Uh—Carver?"

"Yeah, but that's Lieutenant Carver to you, Sergeant."

"Did you talk to Leo, Lieutenant?"

"Briefly. You were attacked? What the hell is going on?"

"Yeah, late last night. I'm okay. Can you give me a few minutes, and I'll be there to fill you in?" he said as he cupped his free hand over his mouth to muffle a yawn.

"How come this is the first time I'm hearing about this?"

"There's a lot going on. I'll tell you all the details in person, okay?"

James walked into the kitchen with bedhead, yawning as he sat at the table next to Malone.

"Lieutenant, my son just woke up. I'll be there as soon as possible."

"Yeah, yeah. Okay."

Malone hung up and looked over at James.

"Hey, pal. You okay? You sleep good?"

James frowned. "I had a bad dream."

"Sorry to hear that." He put his arm around James. "Want some breakfast?"

"Yeah. Cereal."

"You got it. I'll have some cereal with you too. Is Mom up?"

"Think she's in her room."

"Okay—tell you what—let's eat our cereal by the TV."

"Yeah!" James said, plopping down on the floor right in front of the television. "I want some Lucky Charms, with lots of marshmallows."

"You got it. I'm just gonna check on Mom, and then we'll have breakfast."

"Okay, Dad."

Malone knocked on the bedroom door and an awkward feeling came over him. Just a few months ago he lived here, but now he felt like a guest. "Ann—you awake?" he said in between light knocks.

"Are we still in danger?" Ann said as she opened the door, wearing a bright, green t-shirt and dark, blue pajama pants.

Malone didn't say anything.

"Shit. I know what that means."

"—I'll make sure you're safe," he cut in. "Put a squad right outside the house."

"What about you?"

"I'll be fine. Look," Malone said with a sigh. "James is up. I gotta go in soon. Do I still have any clothes here?"

"Let me look around. I'm sure there's something."

"Thanks."

Malone walked down the hall and got the cereal from the kitchen. James was watching cartoons, and Malone put the bowl in front of him.

"You like orange juice on your cereal, right?"

"Noooo!"

"You sure?"

"Milk, Dad!"

"Oh—yeah, right."

He started the coffee and pulled a milk jug out of the refrigerator.

"Here you go," Malone said as he poured the milk on the cereal.

"Dad, you forgot something important."

"Oh yeah," Malone said as he scooped some marshmallows out of his bowl and put them into his son's.

James was grinning from ear to ear, and Malone smiled back. Malone's phone rang with a Chicago number, and he ignored it. They both ate their cereal while watching some cartoons. As Malone finished his bowl, Ann walked into the room carrying a shirt.

"Found this in the closet. I think it'll still fit you."

"Thanks." Malone laid the clean shirt over his shoulder. "I'm gonna have a cruiser right outside the house."

"Okay," Ann replied slowly.

Malone kissed James on the head. "I gotta go, pal. Be real good for Mom, okay?"

James smiled back. Ann hovered near the door and Malone lowered his voice. "You gonna be okay?"

"Are you kidding? People are trying to kill us."

"You wanna stay at your sister's place for a little while? A change of scenery could be a really good thing."

"I dunno."

"Think about it. I know she'd love to see you and James."

"Yeah, maybe. I'll look into it."

"You're gonna be fine. I'm gonna get these bastards. I'll call you later, okay?"

Ann stood there and stared off into the distance, her face lacking emotion.

"Okay." Malone walked to his car. He briefly glanced back at Ann and left.

CHAPTER EIGHTEEN

After Malone changed his shirt in his car and used the rearview mirror to comb his hair with his fingers, his phone rang again with the same Chicago number and the call went to voicemail. He stepped into the station, ducked into the bathroom, and splashed cold water on his face. The long days, long nights and drinking were starting to take a toll. It had been a week since he last shaved, and his beard had more grey specks popping up in it.

Coffee in hand, he knocked on Carver's door. Carver was on the phone but motioned Malone to come into his office. Carver looked mad, or frustrated.

"Yeah, yeah, okay," Carver said to the other voice on the phone. "Look—I gotta go." He hung up the phone. "Stupid bastards," he said. "Mayor wants to cut the goddamn budget again. They were just singing our praises, and now they wanna gut us so we can't do our damn jobs."

"Not that surprising is it?" Malone said. "He's a fucking politician."

"Yeah, you're right. Now, what the hell's going on with you? You thinking you're greenlit?"

"Yeah, no doubt. Maybe the Sinaloa Cartel or the New Gens. Bastard damn near blew my head off at my place, and then another prick tried to gun down my ex and kid while they were asleep."

"You gotta be fucking kidding me. A goddamn cartel hit on a Chicago cop?"

"Looks like it. And whoever it is, they're supplying the Latin Kings."

"The mayor had you by the dope on the table and mentioned you in his damn speech."

"Exactly."

"I guess the underlying question is who haven't you pissed off?"

"Good question. I guess I still got you in my corner, right?"

"You're hanging on by a very fine thread," Carver said. "You got IAD investigating you. And now you've got, what, a few new bodies from last night?"

"Just one. And he did just try to blow my head off."

"I'm telling you—IAD's watching you like a hawk. Stay on the straight and narrow. I don't need to tell you about all the shit stains on your record, do I?"

"Nah, that's okay. But I do want to put a couple guys on my ex and my son. Just for a few days until shit calms down."

"Look Malone, I wanna help you out, but my hands are tied. They just axed the budget to the bone. You want someone on them, it's gonna have to be your ass or someone else on your team."

Malone rolled his eyes and started to say something but stopped himself. "You—uh—got anything else for me?"

"Yeah. We need someone to take Max's place on the GTF. My decision, but I'm open to suggestions."

"Can you wait a week or two? There's too much going on right now. Not a good time to bring on anyone."

"It's never gonna be a good time," Carver said. "Just give me a few names."

"How about Ramirez in Narcotics? Miller's good, too. Either one is fine."

"Okay, I'll make a decision and run it up the ladder. Expect a new member by the end of the week. Now get your ass outta here. Try to keep it in one piece, ya know?"

Malone stood up and got ready to leave.

"I'm serious. Watch your ass, Malone. You're in the middle of a shit storm."

"Yeah. What else is new?"

Malone walked out and saw Johnny getting coffee in the break room. Johnny stepped into the hallway.

"Sorry about what happened last night with you and your ex. How's everyone doing?"

"They're okay. I just need to get a couple guys to keep an eye on them, but I'm getting the usual shit about a tight budget. Got any ideas?"

"Maybe we could get a couple guys from the academy to help out?"

"Guess that's better than nothing."

"I know a few in there. Let me make some calls."

"Thanks. Anything out of the ordinary last night for you?"

"Nope, nothing. It was really quiet."

"You pop the big question?"

"No, not yet. Think I'll give it a little more time."

"I get it. Leo here?"

"Yeah. He's been digging into everything from last night."

Malone and Johnny found Leo hunched over his computer monitor starting at the screen. Malone walked up to him.

"Hey," he said. "Find anything?"

"Yeah. The shooter at your place was identified as Manny Rodriquez. 27 years old. No known criminal record. His residence is 3052 South Harding, right here in town."

"Any ties to gangs or cartels?"

"Nothing confirmed at this time."

"Anything on the torched SUV?"

"No. Nothing solid. It was really dark last night and the fire didn't help either."

"Shit. Maybe we're gonna find something at his place."

"Be nice to step out for a little while," Leo said.

"You gonna hold down the fort?" Malone said to Johnny.

"Yeah, sure."

"Oh yeah, I almost forgot. I got a special project for you." Malone wrote something on a piece of paper. "I'm just gonna leave the directions for you right here."

Johnny glanced at the note: *Look for bugs. IAD has their eye on us.*

"Okay. Um, thanks," Johnny said. "I'll get on this."

CHAPTER NINETEEN

Malone and Leo left headquarters and drove down South Halstead.

"You work all night?" Malone said.

"Some at home after checking out that torched SUV. Then I came in early."

"Thanks for all the shit you've been doing. You've been busting some ass."

"It's not a problem. Seems like it's been quite the shit storm lately, hasn't it?"

"Yeah, they never tell you about all this shit, do they? If they did, be a few less rookies on the force."

"Yeah, no kidding."

"We still don't know what the hell happened. Could be Latin Kings, Sinaloa, or New Gens. What's your gut telling you on this mess?"

"My best guess is the New Gens. But whoever it is, a lot of money, drugs, guns, and egos involved."

Malone nodded in agreement. "Yeah, and they're pissed off. I think what kicked this off was having my ass standing next to the dope on the table."

"I agree. Whoever it is, they think you're at war with them. And they've got no limits. No remorse."

"Yeah, maybe I am at war with 'em." Malone bit his lower lip after the words left his mouth. He never said that out loud before. The thought had been a whisper in his head since Andrew died. When Max died, the whisper turned into a scream. It felt good to say the words, but at the same time, it scared him. He reached into his jacket pocket and took a quick drink.

Malone got out of the car and stuck his hands into his pockets and buried his neck into his shoulders so his coat would block some of the cold air. The Chicago winter seemed to be getting colder, and it was cutting deep.

Malone and Leo walked toward the entrance.

"Looks like a two-flat," Leo said.

"Yeah, I bet a sister or mother has a floor here. Maybe more."

Malone knocked, and an elderly woman appeared by the door. "Mrs. Rodriquez?"

"Sí."

Malone held up his badge. "Déjanos entrar—ahora. Asuntos policiales. Dónde vive Manny?"

"Aqua." The woman pointed up the stairs toward the second floor and motioned for the men to come in.

"Gracias. Solo seremos un momento."

The woman disappeared down the hallway.

"Didn't know you knew Spanish, Malone."

"Yeah. I'm full of surprises. Max taught me some."

"That's good."

The two men searched the room. Malone looked under the bed and in the dresser while Leo searched under the couch and in the kitchen for guns, dope, cash, phones, paper, anything that would present a new lead.

Nothing.

Malone entered the second bedroom and looked under the bed, in the dresser, in the closet.

Nothing.

"There's gotta be something here," Malone said. "I know it. Keep looking."

Malone went into the bathroom and lifted the back of the toilet where he found a revolver and a cell phone sealed in a plastic bag.

"Here we go," Malone said.

"Oh yeah?" Leo said from the kitchen.

"Yep. Looks like we just struck pay dirt." Malone showed Leo the gun and phone.

"Nice. I think I may have found something too. The back of that couch look odd to you?"

"Yeah, it does."

Leo unzipped the couch cushion and found a kilo of heroin from the padding.

"Alright. Let's get out of here," Malone said as he tucked the gun and phone into his coat.

Malone and Leo walked down the stairs and did not see the elderly woman anywhere. The two men got in the car and unzipped their coats and pulled out the dope, gun, and phone.

"Know how long that would have taken if we'd have waited for a warrant?" Leo said.

"Yeah, I know. Ask and ye shall receive. Drive-thru?"

"Sure, let's do that."

"How about a dog at Dan's or Portillo's?"

"Don't matter to me."

Leo pulled the cell phone out of the plastic bag. "Looks like this is a burner," he said as he pressed the power button and the phone turned on.

"And it's still got a charge."

Leo scrolled through the phone menus. "There are four contacts in here, all out of state."

Malone noticed a young black man lying flat on the sidewalk in front of a house. He immediately thought of Andrew's unconscious body in the hospital room. No. Not again.

"Shit, you see that?" Malone said as he pulled over to the side of the road.

"You thinking overdose?"

"Yeah, probably. There's some Narcan in the glove box."

Leo pulled out the inhaler and met Malone on the sidewalk.

"I got a really weak pulse," Malone said.

Leo administered the Narcan. "I think he stopped breathing," he said.

Malone pinched the man's nose and started rescue breathing.

Leo contacted dispatch and gave the location.

"Let's try it again," Malone said.

Leo gave the man another dose of Narcan while Malone continued rescue breathing.

No response.

Leo watched as Malone breathed into the man's mouth.

"Malone?" Leo said. "Malone—he's gone. We got here too late."

Malone continued the rescue breathing.

"He's gone. Who knows how long he's been out here."

Malone looked up at Leo. "Give 'em another dose," he said.

"He's gone," Leo said. "Let it go. You did all you could."

Malone sat there in silence as he looked down at the corpse on the ground. His hands were shaking and he was breathing heavily.

An ambulance pulled up in the street. Malone tried to

block out the sound of the siren. He climbed back into his car, took a drink, and closed his eyes.

Leo filled in the EMTs.

Malone heard the car door open and turned toward Leo.

"They just left," Leo said. "We did all we could. Nothing more we could do."

"Yeah."

"You want to get some food or head back to the office?"

"I ain't hungry."

"You sure you're good to drive? I can drive."

"I'm fine."

Malone saw his phone ring and he let it go straight to voicemail. A few minutes later, his phone rang again. Malone pulled up in front of the station and said, "I'll be there in a few minutes. I need to call my CI back."

"Yeah, no problem," Leo said as he got out of the car and walked into the building.

Malone called the number back without listening to the voicemail.

"Saw you called," he said. "What's up?"

"Need to see ya," Mikey said. "We got somethin' to discuss."

"Is it important?"

"Price of shit's flying through the roof. Doubled overnight."

"No shit. When'd you find this out?"

"Yesterday."

"Why didn't you call me then?"

"Little busy at the time, know what I'm sayin'."

"Supply is down?"

"Think so."

"I need you to get ahold of your brother as soon as fucking possible."

"You kiddin' me? You already shook him up once. Not doing that shit again. I ain't sellin' out my blood."

"Don't give me that shit. You're gonna need more cash if the price of shit is going up. I can help you with that."

Malone waited for Mikey to respond and knew that the silence meant he was thinking things over.

"Alright, I'll see what I can do."

"Make it quick. I gotta meet him in person. You still at the shelter on Ridgeland?"

"Yep."

"Okay. I'll be seeing you soon."

CHAPTER TWENTY

Malone arrived back at police headquarters and found Leo and Johnny both standing in front of a white dry erase board covered with red and green writing.

"Any updates?" Malone said.

"I dropped off the dope and gun at the lab," Leo said as he picked up his coffee mug.

"All four numbers in the phone are inactive. I'm betting those are burners too. The most recent call was two days ago for one minute to a California-based number. The call took place one hour before the run-in at your apartment."

Leo sat down at his desk as Johnny stood in front of the whiteboard with his arms crossed.

"What area code is that California number?"

"San Diego, just like our U-Haul driver."

Malone smiled. "Now we're fucking getting somewhere. My CI is gonna set up another meet with Antoine. I gotta figure out who greenlit me and how to make it stop."

"Hey, Johnny, why don't you get that?" Malone said.

Johnny walked over and picked up.

"Yeah, GTF."

Johnny listened to the voice on the other end of the line.

"Yes, sir, will do."

Johnny hung up.

"Carver wants you in his office right now."

"He say anything else?"

"Nope."

Malone took a deep breath. "We probably have a new team member, or IAD is officially going to fuck us in the ass," he said. "Maybe both. Have some lube ready when I get back."

Both Leo and Johnny chuckled and shifted their eyes back to the words on the whiteboard.

Malone trotted down the hallway and knocked on Carver's office door. As usual, Carver was on the phone and waved him in.

"Yeah, Larry. That's fine. Yeah. Yeah. Yeah. Look—I gotta go."

Malone was already sitting in the chair facing Carver.

"You knew this day was coming," Carver said. "Shit's officially hit the fan."

"Want me to act surprised?"

"Just found out that the city cuts are deeper than we thought. Fifteen percent of the overall police budget."

"And we're on the chopping block, huh?"

"Yeah, looks that way. I'd say it's very likely. Wanted to be the one to tell you. Any complaints or negative press, that'll be the nail in the coffin."

"Heard all of this before."

"I know you're a stubborn son of a bitch. I gotta give you that."

"Anything else?"

"You mentioned that you wanted Ramirez or Miller on your team. Pick one."

"Thought you said we're gone."

"Ain't over til it's over, right? We still have the rest of December. New budget starts in January."

"Got that right. I'd pick Ramirez."

"Fine, consider it done."

"Find out anything about the IAD investigation?"

"Some new up and comer named Theresa Wilson is in charge."

"Sounds like a journalist, not an IAD rat."

"Haven't heard from her?"

"Nope."

"Check your voicemail."

Malone looked down as his phone as he said, "Any more good news?"

"Not at the moment."

"Okay."

Malone got up and started to turn and walk out.

"Malone."

"Yeah?"

"I'm serious. Any negative press seals it. Mind your shit, and maybe you won't end up sitting at a desk pushing around piles of paper all day."

"Yes, sir."

"I ain't kidding. Your ass is on the straight and narrow from now on."

"You know me."

"Yeah, that's the problem."

Malone entered the GTF office and sat down at his desk without saying a word.

Johnny and Leo both looked at Malone, who was now looking up at the ceiling.

"Good news is Ramirez is going to be joining the team. Bad news is they're gutting the whole fucking department," he said. "Fifteen percent cuts across the board in January. Some hotshot named Theresa Warner with IAD is leading the investigation. I think she's been calling me. So watch your ass and don't be surprised when they pop in here at the worst possible time asking a shit-ton of questions."

"You been through an investigation before?" Johnny said.

"Yeah, a couple years ago. A bunch of bullshit questions and attempts to get under my skin. They went away after a while. Thankfully, the rats go away if they ain't got something to eat."

"I got a wife and a kid," Leo said. "A mortgage to pay."

"You ain't alone," Malone replied. "We stick together on this. If we start ratting out each other, we ain't no better than the assholes we arrest every day."

Malone pulled his flask out and took a drink.

"Come on man, you can't be doing that here," Johnny said.

"I agree," Leo said. "Not with all that's going on."

"Okay." Malone poured the rest of the whiskey into a plant in the corner of the office until his flask was empty.

"Happy?"

"I guess. But you know you probably just killed that plant, right?" Leo said with a laugh.

"Damn, I just can't fucking please you guys. Shit, just realized I left my coffee in the car," Malone said, pointing to Johnny and Leo and motioning for them to follow.

"I need some coffee too," Johnny said to Leo. "You want some?"

"Yeah, sounds good."

The three men stepped out of the office and Malone stopped them in the hallway. "That plant would have been a great place to hide a bug, you know?"

Johnny and Leo nodded in agreement.

"We gotta watch everything we say in the office. Hell, your car, even your house could be bugged. If IAD wants someone bad enough, there ain't much they won't do."

"You thinking they are gonna interfere in our investigation? We have a lot on Manny, but we didn't have a warrant," Leo said.

"One thing at a time. You didn't find shit looking for bugs, huh?" Malone said to Johnny.

"Nope. Nothing at all."

"Okay. Keep looking every fucking where. Light fixtures, outlets, cabinet drawers, you name it."

"Yeah, okay," Johnny said.

"Excuse me, Sergeant Malone?" A woman's voice said from down the hall. She had shoulder-length brown hair, dark eyes, and was wearing a black pants suit with a white blouse. She approached with her hand extended. "Teresa Warner of Internal Affairs," she said with a smile.

"Yes, I'm Sergeant Malone," Malone replied as he shook her hand.

"I have some questions for one of you."

"Sure. Glad to help you with that. But can we do it later today?"

"I've tried calling you three times already. I'm starting to think you're avoiding me."

Malone smiled and said, "No, no, no. Just in the middle of a big case and having some personal issues."

"Is that something that is effecting your job performance?" Theresa said dryly.

Malone shook his head no. "Not at all. Is it possible that you could question Officer Kaminski first?"

"I suppose."

"Hi there," Leo said as he extended his hand.

"Theresa Warner," she said as she shook his hand. "Shall we?" Warner motioned with her hand to go down the hall.

"Sure. Is it okay if I get some coffee first?"

"Of course."

The two started to walk down the hall.

Malone watched Leo and Warner walk down the hall and then turned to Johnny.

"Well, we knew this shit was coming."

"Damn. She is really hard to read, ain't she?" Johnny said.

"Sure is. What are we expecting from a fucking rat, you know?" Malone replied.

"This is really messed up," Johnny said with a shaky voice.

"Yeah, it is. I know I told you this earlier, but it's the truth: we get paid to swim in shit. Kinda like the sewer department with guns and badges. Hell, those bastards probably make more than us."

Malone and Johnny went back into the office and started searching for bugs. They looked in light sockets, light fixtures, plants, desks, chairs, staplers, and anywhere else anyone would think to plant a bug. They searched for a few hours, turning the entire office upside down.

"Okay, looks clear, for now," Malone said, "but the less time we spend here, the better off we're gonna be."

Leo walked into the office and sat down at his desk.

"How'd it go?"

"Good, good. No problems at all. I could go for some food, how about you?" Leo then pointed toward the exit.

Malone nodded.

"Sure," Johnny replied.

Once outside of headquarters and in the parking lot, Leo said, "We got a problem. She's really good. Like a goddamn bulldog. She ain't gonna let us go."

"I hear you. But we ain't going down without a fight," Malone said. "Besides, we got an even bigger fish to fry. Let's go on a little field trip."

CHAPTER TWENTY-ONE

Malone slowed the car to a stop behind a school bus and watched as three kids step off the bus at the corner. A teenage boy walked over to them and held out a small bag in his hand. Two ignored the teen and the last one took the bag and continued walking toward the school.

"It's a damn shame here," Johnny said. "These kids ain't got a chance."

"Yeah, you're right."

"This is the place Ramirez mentioned the other day?" Leo said.

"Yep. More activity in this area than ever before. Latin Kings and Gangster Disciples are both pushing for the same turf."

Malone noticed St. Peter's Church further down the block and parked on the street. "Gimme five minutes," he said.

Malone got out of the car and entered the church. He saw a woman step out of the confessional and he went inside. As he opened the door, he saw the shadow of the priest against the screen.

"Is that you, Alex?"

"Yes? Do I know you?"

"Alex, this shit ain't gonna fly."

"Beg your pardon?"

"You heard me."

"I'm sorry, I don't recognize you. Who are you, son?"

"You know who the fuck I am. I'll say it one last time: this shit ain't gonna fly."

Alex leaned forward in his seat.

"Malone?"

"Yeah."

"What's it been—two, almost three years?"

"Something like that."

"What are you talking about?"

"No more selling shit to kids. Run that up the ladder or let me tell 'em myself. I don't give a fuck."

"I—I can't do that."

"Let me then. If something don't change, you're gonna be doing more funerals—for lots of kids."

"Look, I don't have any say about what they're doing."

"Bullshit. This is happening in your goddamn backyard. And I know you're paying them. You're funding the bastards that are poisoning kids."

"If I don't pay they'll come after me, my parishioners. Anything's possible. There's nothing I can do..." Alex's voice was shaky and trailed off.

"You know that's all bullshit. You're just scared."

"I can't—there's nothing I can do."

"Just give me a name. Your contact—whoever the hell you're paying."

"I—umm," Alex dabbed the sweat beading on his forehead.

"Tell me."

"I don't have a name. I just leave some money in my mailbox at the same time each month."

Malone stared through the screen and sized up Alex. He wasn't sure if he was telling the truth or not. He didn't really care.

"You're fucking lying to me. Why the hell are you protecting them?"

"No, I'm not. I'm not. Really, I'm telling the truth."

"We've known each other for a long time. You better be telling the truth. I find out you're fucking lying, I'll be back —understood?"

"Yeah. I understand."

"Good. Run that shit up the ladder. I don't care if you gotta leave a goddamn Post-It note with my fucking number on it. No more selling to kids. Got it?"

"Yeah, I got it."

Malone walked out of the church and got back in the car.

"What were you doing in there?" Johnny said.

"Confession is good for the soul," Malone said.

"Didn't know you were religious."

"I know the priest there. Went to high school together. We just had a little chat."

"You just threaten a priest?" Leo said.

"Just a discussion. A nice, private discussion. That's all."

"I see," Johnny said.

"How about we get something to eat?" Leo said.

"Craving more donuts, huh?" Malone said.

"I'm just saying I could eat something," Leo said.

"I was joking. We'll get something later. We got a little more work to do."

The snow started to come down harder and the swirling clouds of white specks filled the sky. Malone didn't mind the winter; the fresh snow covered up the dirt. He found it a nice distraction from some of the crime. He pulled up in front of the homeless shelter on Ridgeland, knowing it would be packed due to the snow.

"Let's head in here together. Won't take long."

The others got out of the car and followed Malone inside. Malone stopped by the entrance to shake off the cold and stomped his feet by the doorway. An elderly black man smoked a cigarette by the door.

"Hey, Louie," Malone said. "How you doin?"

"Good, Malone. You?"

"Busy fighting the good fight."

"Sounds 'bout right."

"Mikey here?

"Yeah, he's in the corner in his usual spot."

"Thanks. Let me know how many kids you have down here, and I'll swing by on Christmas Eve."

"Great. I'll let you know."

Malone led Leo and Johnny past the rows of cots and mats on the floor. The three men cut through the room until Malone stopped in front of a man covered with a dirty brown trench coat asleep in the corner.

Malone tapped the man on the shoulder. "Mikey, wake up." Mikey slowly moved and opened his eyes to see Malone staring down at him. "Rise and shine."

"Huh?" Mikey rubbed his eyes and yawned. "What's that?"

"Dig you get ahold of Antoine?"

"Sorry, I ain't been able to get ahold of 'em."

"Yeah, yeah. I need to find him now. He's got information I need."

"I'm telling ya, he ain't returning my messages. Can't get hold of 'em."

"Yes, you can—I know it."

Mikey looked up at Malone and rubbed his eyes again.

"Bet you're feeling the urge to shoot up. It's been what,

about 24 hours? Every limb is aching and feeling as heavy as shit. Like you're in quicksand."

"No—naw, I'm a'ight. Just can't get any sleep around this damn place."

"Just tell me where he is, and all your problems go away."

"Shit man. You ain't giving a nigga no choice."

"No, I'm not."

"A'ight, a'ight, man. Last I know he's staying at the house on Ashland by da Southside Motel."

"Why the hell would he be there?"

"Keepin' an eye on the girls. They drop off cash there."

"See that wasn't so hard, was it?" Malone held a plastic baggie with a few pills.

Mikey quickly took it from him and held it in his hands.

"Get up. Get yourself straight, and come outside," Malone said. "You're coming with us."

As they walked out, Johnny said to Malone, "Man, you come in here acting like Santa Clause, and a few minutes later you're giving your CI drugs?"

"Gotta do what we gotta do," Malone said as he put a cigar in his mouth. "Know what I mean?"

"You know that's the kinda stuff IAD would nail us for, right?" Johnny said as he got into the backseat.

"He's got a point, Malone," Leo said. "We got IAD all over us. They could be following us."

"Calm the fuck down. I gave him some caffeine pills. Nothing illegal."

"Really?" Johnny said.

"Yes, really. I don't need him nodding off. I need him awake to help us. Let me ask you guys something. What's the difference between black, white, and grey?"

"That a riddle or something?" Johnny said.

"No," Malone said. "It's the truth. What's black to one

motherfucker is just grey to another." Malone cleared his throat. "And we're living in grey now, like it or not."

"I didn't know you were so poetic," Leo said. "Maybe you just trade that cigar for a pipe and that leather jacket for a sweater."

"Yeah, that's me. A badass Mr. Rogers."

CHAPTER TWENTY-TWO

Mikey wandered out of the church feeling better. Malone met him by the door.

Leo and Johnny were already sitting in the backseat of the car.

"Hop in," Malone said. "We're gonna go talk to your brother."

Mikey opened the door and sat in the passenger seat. "Damn, Malone! Cold in here as it is outside." Mikey cupped his hands around his mouth and blew into them.

"Yeah, yeah. Every now and then the heat works. You're welcome to give it a try."

"Hell yeah I'm gonna give it a try." Mikey turned on the heater, and it blew cold air right at his face.

"Goddamn it, Malone. You an asshole!"

Malone laughed.

"Asshole or not, that was pretty funny."

Malone held his hand up in front of the dashboard. The blowing cold air turned a bit warmer.

"Look at that," Malone said. "Maybe you're good luck."

"But you're still an asshole," Mikey said.

Everyone laughed.

"Which one is it?" Malone said as he slowly drove by a short row of brick houses across from the Southside Motel.

"The first one. Others is empty. Ain't no cars around. My brother ain't there."

"Okay, we'll stop in here for a minute. Figured you'd like a bite to eat." Malone pulled into the parking lot of a McDonald's.

"Yeah," he said. "Sure would."

"Hey, what time is it?" Leo asked.

"It's 3:45," Malone replied. "Got somewhere you need to be?"

"Nope. I was just wondering. Probably too early for any action at the hotel, huh?"

"Man, there's always some action going on," Mikey said.

"We'll grab a bite and head over there," Malone said.

Johnny, Leo, and Mikey followed a few steps behind Malone as they approached the restaurant.

"You guys go on in. I'm gonna finish my cigar and make a phone call." He gave Mickey a ten-dollar bill. "Get yourself something to eat."

Mikey smiled and went in.

Malone puffed on his cigar and watched the cars drive by. He made a call.

"Crime lab, this is Jake."

"Hey, Jake. It's Malone. You find out anything with that heroin?"

"Yeah, was just about to call you. That heroin is uncut. Had to come straight from the source."

"You sure?"

"Yeah, absolutely. Ain't seen something that pure here in quite a while."

"No trace of fentanyl at all?"

"Nope."

"Okay. Thanks for the info."

He hung up, finished his cigar, and stepped inside the restaurant. He saw Leo and Johnny standing by the counter.

"Miss us?" Leo said as he took a sip of coffee.

"Thought I'd get some coffee."

Leo coughed and made a choking sound. "Goddamn. Tastes like an ashtray mixed with some cat piss."

"How do you know?" Malone said with a laugh.

"Here, take mine. I can't drink that," Leo said as he held out the brown paper cup.

Malone took a sip. "Goddamn, that'll put some hair on your balls, won't it."

Johnny smiled and took a bite of a sandwich.

"Watch it, rookie," Malone said, "I saw you laughing at me."

"What?"

"You heard me."

"No, no. I wasn't," Johnny said.

"I'm just fucking with you," Malone said. He joined Mikey sitting at a separate booth a few seats over.

"What'd you get?"

"Burger and fries. Not bad. Not bad at all."

"Want anything else?"

"Naw, I'm good."

"Here," Malone said as he handed over his phone. "Call Antoine again. I need to meet him right now."

"Lemme call him on my burner," Mikey said. "I call him on a cop's phone he gonna be pissed at me forever."

Mikey pulled a phone out of his pocket and dialed.

"He ain't picking up, man. I'll leave him another message."

"Tell'em to call your ass right back," Malone said.

"Hey. It's me. Call me back a'ight? It's important. Got Malone here, and he gotta talk now."

Malone sighed out loud.

"Thanks, man. Hang right here, okay. He calls you back, come and get us."

"Got no problem with that. Freezing out there."

Malone smiled briefly as he watched Mikey eat the rest of his burger. Then he turned and walked toward the door.

Leo and Johnny followed.

Once outside, Malone said, "Crime lab says the heroin from the shooter's place was uncut. Believe that shit?"

"From the cartel?" Leo said.

"Sure looks like it."

"Damn," Johnny said.

The three men walked out of the parking lot. The sky was a slight shade of grey now and the air was even colder. Malone shrugged off the cold and led the way behind the strip mall connected to the McDonald's. They saw a row of small brick houses at the end of the block. The team followed Malone to the first house.

"There could be anyone inside here," Malone said when they got to the back door. "Stay alert, keep your eyes open."

Malone stood in front of the door holding his P226 and pulled a flashlight out of his pocket. He thought about kicking in the door but leaned forward to test the handle. It was open. He went in with Leo and then Johnny following, each holding Glocks and flashlights in their hands.

The kitchen was empty. No dishes in the sink, no obvious recent signs of use. The living room was filled with dated furniture and a TV in the corner. Malone motioned to the others that he was going upstairs. He swallowed hard as his heart beat harder in his chest. The sights were all too familiar. His mouth watered and he fought the urge to vomit as he walked up the stairs.

At the top was a small bedroom with just a bed inside and a hallway that branched off in the other direction.

Johnny motioned to go left. Malone shook his head no

and stepped closer to Johnny.

"No," Malone whispered. "We stay together—got it?" Despite only talking at a whisper level, Malone thought it felt more like a quiet scream coming out of his mouth.

The three men went into the first bedroom with Malone leading the way. He searched the corners and any blind spots, then crouched down to look under the bed.

"Clear."

The others nodded.

"You see this?" Leo said as he turned his flashlight toward a syringe on the small table next to the bed.

"Yeah. Keep looking."

The men continued to search the room but found nothing else.

They went down the hallway toward the other doors. One more door on the left and one on the right at the end of the hall.

Malone followed the beam from the flashlight that led to the door on the left. He carefully opened it. An empty bathroom. Grey walls, a white toilet, a white sink, and an off-white tile floor. Nothing else.

Malone motioned toward the last door at the end of the hallway. He put his hand on the doorknob and slowly opened it. The flashlight beam shone into the pitch dark room, revealing another bed and a nightstand with some empty beer bottles on it. Nothing else.

"This is bullshit," Malone said as he shut the door and turned around. "The bastard would have his car with him."

"Yeah, you're right," Leo agreed.

"What do you wanna do now?" Johnny said as they walked toward the backdoor.

"Funny you should ask," Malone said. "First, we gotta get you some different clothes. And then some booze. You're going undercover."

CHAPTER TWENTY-THREE

Malone slouched in his seat as he watched the parking lot of the Southside Motel. Only junkies and johns with hookers would ever go there. Each person would go in, get their fix and get out, letting the pleasure distract from the fact the place was a complete shit hole. It was this kind of place that made Malone think maybe Vegas had prostitution right; at least those places were safe and not a health hazard.

"Hate this damn place," Malone mumbled under his breath.

"Oh yeah?" Leo said.

"No matter what we do, it's always the same: a non-stop orgy of junkies, hookers, johns, pimps, and gang members. And every second this shit hole is open, it's bringing cash in hand over fist."

"Good training for Johnny though, isn't it?"

"Sure is," Malone said. "How long we been out here so far?"

"About an hour."

Malone pointed his binoculars at the parking lot, scanned

the cars, and looked back at the alley next to the motel. He saw Johnny leaning against the side of the building holding a brown bag.

A dark sedan pulled into the parking lot right next to the motel. A couple of girls walked over and leaned in the car's window. They nodded their heads and shortly after a man with grey hair got out of the car. Together they went into the motel room.

"Shit, you see who that was?" Malone asked.

"The guy who just went in? No, I didn't."

"Think that's James Redford, the City District Attorney."

"No shit."

"Hey. Looks like you've got a new john over there," Malone said into his radio. "Maybe a city official. Keep an eye out."

"Copy that," Johnny said quietly into the radio. He held up the brown bag, pretending to drink.

Malone and Leo kept silent as they watched Johnny wobble out from the alley, stumbling as he moved closer to the motel rooms, with the brown bag in hand.

Malone looked over at Leo who was yawning. "How you holding up?"

"Alright."

"Good."

"You?"

"Hanging in there," Malone was interrupted by Johnny over the radio.

"Just heard someone screaming from that john's room. I'm gonna take a closer look," Johnny said.

"No, hold off. Don't wanna blow our cover," Malone barked.

Johnny continued to move toward Redford's hotel room.

"I said hold off—that's a direct order—got that?"

Johnny set down the brown bag and stood by the door to the room.

"Dammit, he's going in," Malone said as he started the car.

Johnny kicked open the door.

"We gotta get over there," he said. "Now."

Malone pulled up. Leo got out of the car and ran to the room.

A few seconds later, Malone appeared in the doorway. He saw Redford there naked on the bed with a bloody nose. A girl was tied up on the bed, unconscious, and the other was in the corner of the room, both hands covering her face as she sobbed.

"These girls need medical attention," Johnny said. "When I came in, this prick was beating her." He motioned toward the girl in the corner.

Malone walked toward the girl on the bed who looked like she'd been knocked out. He heard shallow breaths. She was definitely still alive.

"Yeah, they do need medical attention," he said. "We'll get it for them as soon as possible. Cuff him and put him in the bathroom. Then fall back," Malone said.

"What?" Johnny said.

"You heard me."

"This is bullshit."

"Did I ask for your input? Just fucking do it," Malone snapped back.

Malone turned back to Leo. "If we didn't step in, he was gonna call 911," he said.

"Yeah, I know—but maybe you should give him a break."

"What the fuck are you talking about?"

"He's new," Leo said. "You said he's trying his best. He just needs some time."

"Yeah, I know," Malone said, "I'm gonna handle this."

"Okay," Leo nodded hesitantly.

Malone walked back into the room and saw Johnny near the door.

"He's in the bathroom?"

"Yeah. He's cuffed in there. Here's the key."

"Okay. Go wait with Leo."

Johnny's eyes widened as he slowly walked out of the room. Malone stepped into the bathroom and saw Redford was naked sitting on the dingy, white tiled floor. His hands were cuffed behind his back.

"You know who I am, right?" Malone asked.

Redford looked up at Malone and nodded his head, muffling something through bloody teeth. Malone leaned down.

"So, tell me, what do you think I want?"

Redford coughed. "D-doesn't matter," he stuttered. "Whatever...you want, you got it." Redford continued coughing.

"Good. Call off the fucking IAD hounds."

Redford nodded his head over and over like he was afraid to stop. Malone held up his phone and took a picture of Redford on the floor.

"Get dressed and go home," Malone said as he uncuffed him. "If I find out either myself or my team is under investigation, I'll be sending the Sun-Times pictures of you, the bruised girls, and your city car parked outside. You know that'll be a popular story. The DA sexually assaulting underage girls. Easy to picture on a front page, ain't it?"

"Fine. Deal. P-please don't tell anyone." Redford's lip quivered as he said the words.

Malone looked down at Redford in disgust. "That's up to you."

Redford slowly got to his feet.

"One more thing," Malone said. "I want you to see these girls get medical attention. Right now."

"How? What...what am I supposed to do?"

"Get creative. I don't care if you have to call 911 from a payphone. Point is, they are getting medical attention right now. Got it?"

"Yeah, okay."

Malone left the room and walked to the alley joining Johnny and Leo.

"Hold up—you're letting him go?" Johnny said. "He was beating the shit out of those girls. They ain't old enough to drive."

"I know. I get it. But I've had enough of your shit." Malone stepped toward Johnny, grabbed his throat, and held him against the building. "You know how they treat cops in jail? It ain't good."

He let go and stepped back as Johnny gasped for air.

"You're—bad as them," Johnny said, winded.

"You don't get it, do you? Shut up for a goddamn minute and let me explain."

Johnny held his hand up and cupped it around his neck as he continued to catch his breath.

"Screw this. I don't wanna hear how you won't arrest a politician. You're full of shit," Johnny said as he started walking away from Malone.

"Wait." Malone grabbed Johnny's shoulder.

Johnny turned around and punched Malone, hitting him in the left eye.

Malone threw back a jab, smacking Johnny on the side of his face followed by an uppercut that sent his head back.

"Stop, stop," Leo ordered, breaking it up. "That's enough." Taking Johnny by the arm, Leo led him away from Malone. "You ain't gotta like it," he said to Johnny, "but you gotta follow orders."

Johnny stood there in a daze. He watched as Malone squinted his left eye.

"Damn kid," Malone said. "You gonna let me explain? I just worked out a deal with Redford. The girls will be getting medical attention right now."

Johnny's eyes widened as he took a few deep breaths.

"He ain't getting away with shit," Malone added. "We'll take care of him after IAD gets off our ass. Get it?"

"Shit, I'm sorry," Johnny said. "I thought you were..."

"Look, I get it," Malone said. "We ain't letting this slide. And you got a helluva right cross." He continued to squint his left eye and rubbed his cheek.

"Had a lot of practice," Johnny said. "You okay?"

"Yeah. You used to be a boxer or something?"

"Nope. Just grew up with a few older brothers."

"You got heart, kid. Just need to mix in some patience."

Malone pulled out his flask. The whiskey soothed him as the smokey flavor filled his throat. He held it out to Johnny who took a drink.

"Think you just popped your cherry," Malone said as he got the flask back from Johnny. "Guess you're officially part of the team."

"Didn't know it'd be so painful," Johnny said with a chuckle.

Malone laughed. "First time ain't no fun."

"Seriously," Johnny said as he held his hand up to the side of his face.

Malone pointed to the house across the street, which now had a light on upstairs. "Looks like someone's home now."

"Cool if I hang back here?" Johnny said.

"Yeah, just watch the front and keep an eye out."

P226 in hand, Malone approached the back door and kicked it in without hesitation. With Leo behind him, he scanned each room carefully. He stopped and motioned Leo up the stairs. Malone then stormed up the stairs with Leo covering his back.

All three doors upstairs were still closed. Malone pointed at one on the left and kicked it in. He broke through and found Mikey inside on the bed, eyes glazed over and not moving.

"Shit," Malone said. He stepped forward and put his hand under Mikey's nostrils.

"Is he...," Leo asked.

"Looks like an overdose. His breathing is really shallow." Malone tried to shake him awake. "Wake up man. Come on, wake the fuck up."

No response.

"Think there's some Narcan in the car," Malone said. "Watch his breathing."

"Yeah. If he stops breathing, I'll do CPR."

Malone ran outside and saw Johnny sitting in the passenger seat. Johnny rolled down the passenger window.

"What's up? I ain't seen nothing out here."

"Need some Narcan. Check the glovebox."

"Overdose?" Johnny said as he flipped open the glove box.

"Yeah. Looks like it."

"Here you go," Johnny said as he got out of the car and handed over the box to Malone. Johnny fell forward in front of Malone as a loud noise rang out.

Malone saw the blood splatter and spray in his direction.

"Shit—no!" Malone fell down, dropping the Narcan on the ground. He crawled forward and opened the passenger door for cover. He looked back and saw Johnny's bloody body in the snow. Malone hurried over to him. Johnny was gone.

"Motherfucker!" Malone felt something hit his arm and knock him back to the ground. He stayed crouched down and saw more blood in the snow, realizing he'd been shot in the left arm, right before the shoulder. He stayed by the car, carefully took off his belt, and tightened it to slow the bleeding.

He heard more gunshots ring out from behind and saw it was Leo, firing his Glock at the building across the street. Malone quickly glanced up to see a flash of gunfire from the roof of that building.

"Officer down!" Leo yelled into his radio. "Officer down! Shots fired! Need an ambulance now! 6100 block by North Jersey Ave. Shooter on the roof."

More shots rang out. One hit Leo in the chest. Malone saw him drop the radio and fall down into the snow.

"Fucking shit!" Malone yelled. He jumped up and pulled Leo to cover next to the car.

He saw the blood pool on Leo's shirt. "You're gonna be fine," he said. "You hear me? Stay with me. You're gonna fucking be alright." Leo didn't respond. "They're on their way. I'm right here man. You're gonna be okay. You're gonna be okay."

Leo whispered something and Malone moved his ear closer to hear.

"Go get the damn shooter," Leo managed. "I'll be fine."

"No fucking way. I ain't leaving you." The gunfire stopped as sirens filled the air.

"Go now," Leo said. "Get him."

"You sure?"

"Yeah. Go."

Malone knew he was right. He waited a few more seconds before moving away from cover, looking briefly at the apartment building across from the motel.

Malone felt nauseous again but kept moving toward the apartment building. The more his body told him to stop moving, the more he refused to listen.

He briefly closed his eyes as he walked and opened them a moment later. He figured it had been about three minutes

JIM WOODS

since the last shot. He got to the stairway and watched for any signs of movement. The shooter was likely still in the building. It was just a matter of finding him.

His arm throbbed, but he didn't care. All that mattered was finding whoever just shot up his entire team.

CHAPTER TWENTY-FOUR

As Malone started to climb the stairs, his arm felt heavier and it was going numb. He took some deep breaths and kept climbing. His feet moved from one stair to the next until he tripped and tumbled forward on the stairwell. He laid there as he tried to gather his thoughts. Malone growled in anger as he got up, more determined than ever. He reached into his jacket pocket looking for his flask but realized it was in the car. Instead of trying to block the pain now, he embraced it and let it take over, using it to fuel him and keep focused. He knew the only thing that would make him feel better was the satisfaction of catching this bastard and nailing his ass to the floor.

Malone smiled as the thought came to mind, then realized he was by the top floor. He breathed heavily and slowed his pace as his thoughts flashed to Max, then Johnny, and then Leo.

The door leading to the roof was unlocked. He reached into his pocket, pulled out his flashlight, and switched it on. He stepped out with his P226 drawn. He tried to move as cautiously as possible, watching and listening for anything out of the ordinary. The roof was wide and had only one access point in the middle. He searched for footprints in the snow and followed the beam of his flashlight.

Nothing.

Fuck.

The shooter definitely wasn't on the roof. He must have been firing from an apartment window. Malone turned off his flashlight and started back down the stairs.

Every movement required even more energy. His breath got heavier in his chest as he moved slowly.

This is bullshit. Not gonna let this happen to the entire team. They don't get to win.

His foot started to wobble as he shuffled down the stairs. He steadied himself and kept moving, knowing that once he stopped moving, that would be it. Malone kept a tight grip on the handrail and was breathing heavily.

His mind drifted as he thought about what had happened. Run-ins with gang bangers with handguns and the occasional AK47 was the norm. A shooter with a sniper rifle wasn't, let alone one that was targeting the entire GTF. Malone figured it must have been a sicario, a mercenary hired by the cartel. Maybe even former military. The cartel had to have more local connections, maybe even a few cops on the payroll to pull these kinds of strings.

He reached the bottom of the stairway and sat down to recover his strength. He checked his phone and saw a missed call from Ann.

"Hey—how are you doing?" he asked. "How is James?"

Ann was silent and then took a deep breath. "How the hell do you think we are doing?"

Malone swallowed hard. "Yeah. I'm sorry to hear that."

"Are you okay? You sound off."

"Just shitty reception. I'm okay."

"James has been having nightmares. I think he's afraid to sleep. And he keeps asking about you."

"Is he up now?"

"Let me see..."

Malone heard Ann walk across the house and open the bedroom door.

"He's half awake." She handed the phone to James. "Here's Dad."

"Hello?" James said.

"Hey, buddy. You okay?"

"Yeah, Dad."

"Good. Sleep well, okay? I love you."

"Night. I love you."

Ann took the phone back. "You caught him with droopy eyelids," she said.

Malone smiled. "Thanks." He leaned forward on the step. "Why don't you go to your sister's for a while, stay over there?"

"James has preschool. I've got my work."

"Just for a few days. Let me clean things up, then you can come back in a little while. Look...I...my team...is all over this. Just give me a week and things'll be different."

Ann took another deep breath. "What the hell is going on?"

"Just do what I'm saying, please?"

"This is bullshit, Ryan. Tell me."

"There...was another shooting."

"What happened?"

"I'm okay. Just promise me you'll get the hell out of town by tomorrow at the latest, okay?"

"Okay. We'll leave."

"Good."

He hung up and sat there for another moment. He carefully pulled his jacket off of his left arm to see the damage. It looked clean like the bullet went right through his arm. He slowly pulled the jacket back on and used the railing to get back up. He was exhausted, but he didn't care. He knew he had no choice but to keep moving, pushing every possible lead.

He walked back over to the stash house. It was now surrounded by police cars and yellow police tape barriers on the sidewalk. He approached a beat cop he knew named Jackson.

"Hey, Malone," Jackson said. "Just found your radio on the ground. Where the hell were you?"

"Shooter on the roof at the apartment building. Think he's gone, but I need you to go over there and take a few uniforms with you. Search the building for evidence. Shooter had a high-powered rifle. A semi-automatic. I need to know what you find out."

"You shitting me?" Jackson said.

"Nope. Did EMS take 'em over to Mercy?"

"Yeah, they left a few minutes ago. You feeling okay? You look really pale."

"Yeah, I'm just fucking tired."

"I'll need your help filling out a report," Jackson said.

"Yeah, okay. You wanna drive me over to Mercy, and I can start working on the report in the car?"

"You bet."

Malone started filling in the report but fell asleep and woke up when the car stopped. He found himself in front of his apartment.

"You fell asleep hard in the car," Jackson said. "Just go get some rest. I'll finish the report."

"Thanks. Yeah, okay."

Malone entered his apartment and pulled a bottle of

painkillers out of the cabinet. As he washed down a handful of pills with whiskey, he took a closer look at the wound and wrapped his arm with white gauze. It still hurt like hell, but nothing more than it should. Then he propped himself up on the couch with pillows and drank until he fell asleep.

CHAPTER TWENTY-FIVE

The next morning, Malone woke up with a hangover and in pain. He tried to piece together what exactly happened and was met with more questions and an arm that felt like it had been crushed by a boulder.

"Motherfucker!" he screamed when he got off the couch to go to the bathroom.

Each movement took more effort than it should and made him feel like he was moving in slow motion. He looked over at his phone on the table and saw he had 10 missed calls. He listened to a voicemail from Carver saying Leo was in ICU. He then scrolled through his contacts, found Morgan's name, and dialed.

The call rang several times and then he heard a woman's voice.

"Hello?" she said.

"Hey. It's Ryan Malone. I need your help."

"What kind of help? Last time you called me, one of your informants got shot."

"Well...uh..."

"Goddammit, Ryan. Is your hand still messed up?"

"No—uh—my arm. I have a gunshot wound close to my shoulder."

"Who the hell do you think you are?"

"Look, I can pay you double what I paid you last time."

"This ain't about money. This is bullshit. You don't do this to someone."

"Yeah. Sorry about that."

Malone coughed and quietly moaned in pain.

"Fine, Malone. But you're an asshole. And because of that, feel free to make it triple. I just worked a ten-hour shift and now I'm missing my beauty sleep."

"Fine."

"Tell me about the wound."

Malone looked at his shoulder. "Left arm, a few inches down from the shoulder. Think it's a clean through and through."

"Are you sure?"

"I think so."

"Okay, I'll be there in about half an hour."

"Alright."

Malone exhaled as he hung up. He knew this was the only way he could be back on the street soon. Going to the hospital would mean taking time off. Carver would be pissed that he didn't stay at the crime scene yesterday. Homicide wouldn't be happy either, but he never got along with them. They were a bunch of detectives that thought they were ten times smarter than they were. Fredo Corleones on power trips. Malone kept everything in-house. What happened in GTF stayed in GTF. At least while there was still a GTF.

Malone decided to call Carver for damage control. The call went to voicemail, and he wasn't sure if that was a good or bad sign. He never called Carver. It was always the other way around.

"Lieutenant, it's Malone. I'm okay. I'm getting my shit

together from yesterday. I'll be seeing you soon, probably later today."

The voicemail was ambiguous enough that it wouldn't put up any red flags, and it was also not too far from the truth. Malone played back the message and it sounded pretty good, even more impressive with a hangover and a gunshot wound.

He staggered to the kitchen and found a box of Pop-Tarts in the cabinet and quickly ate one. He couldn't remember how long it had been since he last ate anything. He made some coffee and ate another Pop-Tart, this time dipping it into the coffee. He started to feel a little better, and the caffeine took away some of the fogginess from the hangover.

As he stood in the kitchen drinking a second cup, he heard a knock on the door. He knew who it was from the knock. He opened the door.

"Geez, Malone," Morgan said. "You look like shit."

"Well, thanks."

Morgan had shoulder-length black hair, deep blue eyes behind glasses, and a smile that could light up a room if she wanted.

"Okay, sit your ass down so I can take a look at you," she said.

"I made some coffee."

"You make shitty coffee." Morgan set her bag on the floor and pulled out several small bottles, some gauze, and tweezers.

"It ain't that bad," Malone said. "How're you?"

She examined the wound. "Helluva lot better than you. Why do you like to go out and get shot so damn much?"

"Not my idea. Guess there are a few assholes in Chicago that wanna take a crack at me."

"I believe that," Morgan said in a serious voice and then smiled. "Sounds like most of the dates I've been on."

Malone laughed but moved his arm and it hurt like hell.

"Fuck!"

"Oh, come on now. Tell you what, bite down on this so I can get a closer look and clean your wound."

Malone stuffed part of a red handkerchief into his mouth and bit down.

"Ready?"

Malone nodded as she put her fingers on Malone's arm to examine the wound and take a closer look.

Malone growled through the handkerchief.

"Almost done," she said as a strand of hair fell down across her eyes. She brushed it away with her hand.

"Well, you're right," she said. "It's clean through. Just gotta clean it up so it doesn't get infected. Looks like you'll survive after all."

Malone took the handkerchief out of his mouth.

"Good. I gotta hit the streets today. Can you help me with that?"

"Today? Hell no. You need rest. Take the damn day off."

"I gotta get the assholes who did this. They shot two other guys on my team. If I wait, I might not find the bastards."

"Shit," Morgan said. "I'm sorry. Okay. Let me give you something to keep you on the streets. Make a deal with me?"

"Maybe."

"Once you get those assholes, you need to rest up and heal properly."

"Yeah."

"And you can't drink with this stuff I'm giving you, or it'll mess you up big time. You'll be more likely to shoot your dick off than catch any bad guys. This is the strongest shit you can get. Don't take any more than what I'm giving you. Got that? No drinking until at least 72 hours after you've stopped taking the drug."

"What is it?"

"It's a synthetic drug. A painkiller called fentanyl."

"Hell no. That shit kills people. It causes overdoses all over the fucking place. Ain't that shit used to take down elephants?"

"You're right. It's not safe if you're getting it on the street. People have no idea how much they are taking. I'm giving you a specific dose, not selling baggies on the corner. And I don't know about the elephant thing."

"No way, I can't...not that shit."

"Look. If you wanna get out there today, this is how you gotta do it. Do you trust me or not?"

Malone stared back at her blue eyes. She was sure. Malone sighed out loud.

"Okay," he said. "But this is bullshit."

"I said the same damn thing driving over here."

Malone smiled.

"Now, what'd I say about drinking?"

"Don't drink anything. Not a drop."

"I know you're hungover, but you gotta stay sober. One drink while you're on this shit and you'll be a goddamn train wreck."

"I've had painkillers with alcohol before."

"Not like this. You gotta choose." She held the flask in one hand and the Fentanyl in the other. "Pick one."

"Looks like I ain't got a choice," Malone said as he pointed to the syringe.

"Good. I'm just going to hold onto this for a while," Morgan said and slipped the flask into her coat pocket. "Don't take any more than it says, or you're gonna be spending time in a hospital bed. Here's everything you need."

She held out the syringe and the small bottle.

"Can you give me the first dose?" he asked. "Not a huge fan of needles."

"Is that right? Might explain why you don't have any tattoos."

"Everyone has their limits, right?"

Morgan carefully filled the syringe, tapped out the air bubbles, and pressed the plunger, injecting the fentanyl into his arm.

"Okay, you'll be good for the next few hours. The drug should help a lot. You may feel nauseous or a little dizzy. Give yourself at least an hour or two before you drive."

"This is for you," Malone said as he handed over an envelope with cash.

"Thanks. Now go get the bad guys, okay?"

Malone smiled.

Morgan smiled back and walked out of the apartment.

CHAPTER TWENTY-SIX

Over the next hour, Malone started to feel better and could move around his apartment with minimal pain. He walked in circles from the kitchen to the living room over and over as he thought things through.

The shooter was sent by the cartel. Gangs weren't that professional. He knew he wasn't going to figure out anything there. He went into his bedroom, carefully slipped his body armor over his head, put on a shirt, and zipped up his leather jacket. The vest would be found in a pat-down, but otherwise, it was pretty hard to spot under the jacket. Malone finished off a lukewarm cup of black coffee and decided it was time to hit the streets.

A sense of dread came over him as he walked along South Halstead. He swallowed hard. He felt like he was fighting a losing battle, an unknown enemy that couldn't be defeated. Malone remembered what he told Johnny about Jordan lighting up the Knicks. He ignored the feeling, got into his car, and turned the key. He took a couple of deep breaths as he pulled out on the street.

At a stoplight, he pulled Marty's business card out of his wallet and called the number. It rang repeatedly and the voicemail came up.

"Hello? Yeah, I test drove a truck the other day, just wanted to follow up with you about it. I'll call again later."

Malone hung up and swallowed hard. Maybe Marty just missed the call, but the timing seemed off. He looked down at his watch. 2 o'clock. It was the middle of the afternoon, probably too late for lunch. He thought about driving over there but didn't want to spend two hours going to Milwaukee and back.

Malone noticed his phone ringing.

"Yeah, Malone."

"Hey, it's Jackson. Just wanted to check in on you. How you feeling?"

"Pretty good. You been to the hospital?"

"Yeah, didn't see you down there. Everyone's asking where you are."

"I can't. Not right now. I'll come down as soon as I can though."

He drove around town for about an hour and found himself by the Purple Monkey. He pulled into the parking lot and remembered the last time he was there, half expecting to see Max open the door and step into the parking lot.

Malone noticed a yellow car in the corner of the parking lot and remembered it was Vi's car and went inside the building.

A tall blonde danced on stage and a redhead tended the bar while a brunette delivered drinks to the handful of customers scattered among the tables. Malone sat down by the bar and gazed at the bottles on the wall.

The bartender came over. "What'll it be?" she asked.

"Is Vi here?"

"Umm, yeah. Think she's in the back giving a private dance."

"Thanks."

"What'll you have?"

"Club soda," he finally said.

"Sure."

The bartender gave him his drink, and he turned his back to the bar. The blonde on stage spun on a pole and flipped upside down while a Def Leppard song played over the speakers. He saw a guy walk past the velvet rope as he left the private rooms. Vi stepped out with a bright purple boa on her arms. Malone approached her.

"Hey," he said. "Can I get a private dance?"

"Sure, darling."

Malone followed her back to a private room. "Do you remember me?" he asked. "I'm Max's friend."

"Oh, yeah. How's he doing?"

Malone sat down in the chair. "He was shot—uh—few days ago. Didn't make it."

"No shit. I'm so sorry. He's really gone?"

"Yeah. That's why I'm here."

"Oh?"

"Remember the guy we had you give a private dance —Antoine?"

"Yeah."

"You seen him since then?"

"No. But I think he mentioned he was leaving town for a few days. He was bragging about some new place he had on the beach."

"Really? He say where it was?"

"Maybe it wasn't him. I hear that story all the time. You know how it goes."

"Yeah. I know Max would want you to have this," Malone said as he handed over some cash to Vi.

"No—no. Please. I'm so sorry about Max."

"Yeah," he said. "Me too."

Malone walked out of the Purple Monkey and his mind started to wander as he considered the new information. He sat in silence as he scrolled through his contacts.

"Hey, it's Malone. Can you meet me for a drink?"

CHAPTER TWENTY-SEVEN

Malone arrived at Dugan's Irish Pub and saw an older gentleman drinking Guinness at a table. The man waved and Malone sat down across from him.

"Hey, Jerry. Thanks for meeting me. How ya doing?"

"Not too bad."

"Good. You hear what's going on downtown?"

"Naw, I stay out of that. Worry more about catching fish and drinking good beer."

"Don't blame you. I need some advice. I'll keep it short. And I'm buying."

"Yeah, no problem."

Malone waved over the waitress.

"What can I get you boys?" she asked.

"One more of whatever he's having, and I'll take a club soda," Malone said.

"Club soda? Really?"

"Doctor's orders."

"I see. Whaddya wanna know?"

"Someone has me and the GTF greenlit. Not sure who it is. They've already tried to take me out a couple times."

"What do you know?"

"Think it's a cartel. Sinaloa or Jalisco New Gens. Not sure which one."

"Shit, I'm sorry," Jerry said. "You know, the thing about cartels is they ain't just about business. They're about fear. They don't just kill you. They come after your family and make a goddamn show of it."

"I know. But it seems like I'm the focus of this mess," Malone said. "Like they're just circling around me. This make any sense to you?"

"Sounds like you pissed off a gang that wants to get in bed with the cartel. Otherwise, you'd have dead bodies lined up in your front yard, including yours. Those pricks'll do anything for shock value."

"A pro opened fire on us by a stash house yesterday," Malone said. "A goddamn professional."

"You sure it was a pro?"

"Yeah. He seemed like a fucking Marine. The bastard shot up the whole damn team with a semiautomatic sniper rifle."

'You know, I heard the New Gens were hiring former military snipers. Even hunting down cops and their families...'

Jerry got quiet and put his hand on his chin.

"But something's missing," he said. "What the hell are you leaving out? What happened before all this shit started?"

"Couple days ago, a deal went sideways. Ended up taking out a few Latin Kings and a cartel runner."

"That's it. In their minds, you declared war."

"No, they fired at us and wouldn't stand down."

"It don't matter."

"It was just three low-level Latin Kings and a cartel runner."

"That's only part of it," Jerry said. "There's something much bigger: you're slow down the flow of drugs into one of the biggest cities in the world."

"Shipments come in all the time."

"Yeah, but they're sending a message. Mess with 'em and you're dead. You can't stop business."

"Yeah."

"Is your family safe?"

"Yeah, staying out of town with her sister."

"Good." Jerry took a sip of his beer. "You got two good options. The smartest move is to back off a little. Lay low for a while."

"What's plan B?"

Jerry licked his lips.

"Try cutting a deal with the Gangster Disciples or Vice Lords. Give 'em some space and in return they keep the Kings busy. Pretty much all you can do."

"Anything else?"

"What do ya mean?"

"They don't get to win. They tried to take me out. Tried to kill my family. Shot up the entire team. I'm not letting this shit happen."

"I get it. Well, as long as you're breathin, this thing ain't over. Keep your nose clean and be ready. These snakes ain't just gonna go away."

"True." Malone closed his eyes and held his right hand up to his temple. "How the fuck did all this happen?"

"You're a fucked-up guy in a fucked-up situation," Jerry said. "What'd you expect? Part of the job."

"Yeah. Tell me, you been in this kind of shit storm before?"

"Oh yeah. More times than I can count."

"How'd you get out of it?"

"What says I ever did?" Jerry said with a smile. "You ain't a real cop until you got countless assholes pissed off at ya."

Malone smiled slightly and waved over the waitress. "Hey

darling, gimme a shot of some—uh—never mind. Get another round for my friend here."

"Sure thing."

"Thanks again," Malone said as he laid down a couple of twenties. "I gotta run."

"Yeah, take care, Malone."

Malone knew backing off wasn't an option. He had to do the only thing he knew how to do.

He could feel the eyes of the other officers on him as he entered the station but chose to ignore it. He just nodded his head and said thanks to anyone who offered their condolences.

Malone sat down at Leo's desk and sifted through the stack of files. Over the last few months, the activities of the Gangster Disciples had been on the decline. The Vice Lords were on the rise and were flagged by Leo for a couple of murders in the last month. Latin Kings had seen the most traction; they were expanding and growing exponentially all over Chicago.

Malone tucked a couple of Latin King files under his arm and left the office. As he walked through the glass door, he saw Carver in front of the building.

"Lieutenant," Malone said.

"Surprised I didn't see you over at Mercy."

"I couldn't do it yet. Seems like I was just there for Max."

"Yeah. I know. I just spoke with his Johnny's family."

"Shit," Malone said, choked up. "He was a good kid."

"Definitely. I do have some good news: Ramirez is on board now with GTF. Get ahold of him and brief him."

"Yeah," he said. "Will do."

"Got anything on the shooter?"

"Not yet from last night. The one at my place was likely a hired gun. No clear gang ties, probably cartel-related. Found some pure heroin in his residence."

"Goddamn it, Malone," Carver said each word slowly. "Whenever I think the shit storm is over, even more shit flies into the air."

Malone nodded.

"Whatever the hell it is you're doing, make it fast," Carver said.

"Yessir, will do."

"I mean really goddamn fast. 24 hours and the clock started 12 hours ago."

"Okay." Malone turned to walk away, then stopped.

"Hey, Lieutenant..."

Carver looked up from the paper in front of him.

"Yeah?"

"When you were at Mercy did you happen to hear anything about my CI, Mikey? OD'd on heroin."

"I thought you'd heard. He didn't make it. I'm sorry."

"Shit. I—uh—thought he was gonna make it," Malone said as he walked away from the station.

CHAPTER TWENTY-EIGHT

Malone pulled out his phone, scrolled to Ann's name, and let his finger hover over the call button. Something inside stopped him, and he put his phone back in his shirt pocket. As he got out of the car, he heard his phone ring and saw Morgan's name flashed on the screen.

"Hey," he said.

"How you feeling?"

"I'm okay, I guess."

"You being straight or are you shitting me?"

"My arm ain't too bad at the moment. The shit you gave me definitely works."

"Good. Remember, no drinking at all. You do and you might as well try to screw an electric outlet."

"Good to know. Don't want to fry anything off."

"Right. Keep that stub you've got."

"Hey, what the hell?" Malone said with chuckle.

"Just kidding. Take care, Malone."

"Hey, Morgan..."

"Yeah?"

"Anything you can do for lightheadedness?"

"You feeling dizzy?"

"Yeah, just a little. You at work?"

"Yeah, I'm on break. I got something I can give you."

"Okay, I'll see you in a few."

Malone drove to Mercy and met Morgan in the parking lot. She gave him some samples and Malone decided to go inside for a minute. He found Leo's wife Debbie asleep in the lobby, using her coat as a pillow. Malone sat down across from her and Debbie opened her eyes.

"Shit, didn't mean to wake you up," he said.

"It's okay."

"Hear anything new?"

"If they can stabilize him, he'll be moved out of here. He's been touch and go for the past twelve hours. But it's okay. I know he'll pull through. He's tough."

"Yeah, he sure is."

"There was nothing you could do differently, was there?" Debbie asked.

Malone hung his head and stared down at the white tile.

"No, no. Nothing different."

He looked up and leaned forward in his chair. "I'm gonna get the bastards that did this. I promise you that."

"I know you will. That's where you've been, right?"

"Yeah."

"So the fact you're here means you hit a dead end?"

"I'm sorting things out."

"You can go see him, you know."

"I can't... I can't."

"Just for a minute. I know it'd mean a lot to him."

"Okay. Just for a minute." Malone's voice was weak and the words didn't want to come out.

Debbie got up and Malone followed her to Leo's bed. As he walked into the room, he got choked up. It looked just like Andrew's room. The same windows. The hospital bed. The same creme-colored walls. The same smell of bleach and disinfectant. The same beeping sounds. Each one flooded his senses, reminding him of death.

"Look who's here," Debbie said.

"Hey man," Malone said, but couldn't find the words to finish the sentence. He shifted his eyes to the floor and just stood there. Something inside wouldn't let him look directly at Leo. He knew if he looked at him, he would lose it. First Max, then Johnny, then Mikey. Now Leo.

"I—I gotta go," he said. "Please let me know if anything changes."

Malone left the hospital and his arm was starting to hurt again. He knew he needed another dose if he wanted to keep going. He tried to remember the last time he slept but his mind was blurry. The line between the last few days was like trying to remember lines in an old movie. Some of the moments were familiar, but most just meshed together.

Malone called Ann.

"You alright?" he asked.

"Yeah. At Amy's place. Doing okay."

"Good. How's James doing?"

"Misses you. He's bored and keeps asking about you."

"Yeah, I bet. Look, it's almost over. I gotta go. I'll talk to you soon."

He put his phone back in his jacket pocket and took his right hand off of the steering wheel. He parked on the street and slowly walked toward his apartment, then hesitated to open it as he saw the hole in the door from the other night.

When he stepped inside, he took the bottle of fentanyl off of the bathroom sink, filled the syringe with the dose, and tapped out the air bubbles. Using his right hand, he rolled up his left sleeve and steadied himself with a few deep breaths. He missed the vein on the first two tries, but found it on the third and pressed down on the plunger.

A few minutes later, the numbness gave him some relief and blurred his thoughts in the back of his mind. He was overcome by a sleepy stillness that made him want to lie down on the couch. Soon his eyes were closed, and he was fast asleep.

———

He woke a couple of hours later in his apartment as his phone lit up with an unknown Chicago number.

"Yeah?"

"Hey. Malone. It's Debbie. Leo's taken a turn for the worse. You asked me to call."

"Shit—yeah. I'll be right there."

Malone threw his coat on and ran out the door. He sped over to the hospital and found Debbie in the corner of the waiting room and sat down next to her.

She looked up at Malone. "The doctor just came out and said that they had to take him back into surgery," she said. "I think they said he has some severe internal bleeding."

Malone reached out and put his arm around Debbie. "He's a tough bastard—you know that," Malone mumbled out loud.

As time passed, Malone half-watched the TV on the other side of the lobby and sunk in his seat, closing his eyes and falling into a light sleep. He woke up to the sound of footsteps of a doctor approaching Debbie.

"Mrs. Kaminski?"

"Yes?"

"I'm Dr. Levin. I'm...sorry, but he didn't make it through surgery. There was just too much internal bleeding."

"No! No!" Debbie screamed as she fell toward the doctor who stopped her from tumbling to the ground.

Malone said nothing, then kicked out one of the chairs behind him. He then flipped over a small, chocolate-colored end table. Security guards came into the lobby to restrain him. "I'm a goddamn cop," he barked as he tore away from them. "Get the fuck off me!"

"You'll have to leave the facility, sir," one of the security guards said as he moved forward, grabbing Malone's arm.

"Get your fucking hands off me," Malone said as he jerked out of the security guard's hands. "Stupid piece of shit."

Malone charged down the hallway and saw Ramirez walk in through the revolving door.

"He's fucking gone," Malone said.

"Wait—where you going?"

Malone kept walking.

"Malone? Malone?" Ramirez ran after Malone and stopped in front of him.

"Wait—wait. Tell me what you're doing. Let me help."

"Nothing you can do."

"That's bullshit and you know it. Where the hell are you going?"

"These fucking pricks ain't getting away with this."

"Wait, you got a new lead?"

"Not yet. "

"Call me when you figure something out, okay?"

Malone didn't reply as he got into his car and then shut the door and drove off.

"Crazy bastard," Ramirez mumbled to himself.

Malone flipped through the file for Hector Torres, also known as Casper. As he stared at the black and white photos, he remembered something Antoine told him earlier.

Kings are greedy. Disciples are smart.

Hector was the manager of KillJoy Tattoo and the shop was in the neutral zone. If the Kings were expanding they would likely have a presence there. It was a long shot, but it was worth trying. Malone pulled out his phone and called Ramirez.

"Hey. I'm at Killjoy Tattoo. Manager has some Latin King ties. Wanna meet me over here?"

"I'll be right there," Ramirez said. "Gimme ten minutes."

"Yeah, okay." He hung up and lit a cigar while he continued to look at the file for a few minutes. "Fuck this," Malone said as he threw the folder on the passenger seat. He then shifted his eyes to the door at the tattoo parlor. No one had gone inside or come out. He wanted a drink but remembered what Morgan had told him and smiled as he shook his head.

He tried to enjoy his cigar, but his nerves wouldn't let him. He was the last man standing from the GTF. He closed his eyes and quickly opened them up again. All he could think of was death. He was surrounded by it. Swimming in it. Living in it.

He took a deep breath and put out his cigar in the ashtray. He checked his watch and saw that five minutes had passed. He got out of the car, went around to the trunk, and pulled out the shotgun. He tucked it under his jacket, crossed his arms, and turned his back to the wind.

"Fuck are you, Ramirez?" Malone mumbled out loud as he secured his body armor under his shirt. He felt better as he loaded and cocked the shotgun. He tucked the shotgun under his jacket as he crossed the street. The paper trail would never show it, but the Kings knew how to get what they wanted. Forcing a business into cooperating was never a problem.

Malone entered the building and immediately got a dirty look from a tattoo-covered man working on a trail of birds on the back of a thirty-something woman. He pulled the tattoo gun off of her back.

"Hell you want?" he asked.

Malone held up his badge. "Is Hector here? I just wanted to chat with him for a minute."

"He sold the place. New ownership. Get the hell out of here."

Malone walked toward the man. "You got a problem?"

"Yeah. I don't like fucking cops." The man continued working on the woman's back.

"Hey," Malone said. The man looked up. Malone hit him square in the face with a right hook and knocked him off the stool. He dropped the tattoo gun on the floor, and the woman screamed.

Malone ignored her and walked toward the back of the store where he saw a door in the far corner. It was locked. He drew his shotgun to use it on the door but something hard hit him in the back of the head. He tumbled to the floor, out cold.

CHAPTER TWENTY-NINE

Malone woke up with a blindfold covering his eyes. Something hard pressed on his back. A metal folding chair. His wrists were tied behind his back and had no give.

"Look who's up," a voice said in the dark. The sound of metal on metal, followed by hissing and blowing.

Malone saw a flickering light getting closer. A blowtorch.

Malone tried to work the ropes around his wrists as the hissing grew louder. Nothing. Thoughts and images flooded his mind.

Ann.

James.

Max.

Johnny.

Leo.

Mikey.

Everything he'd been through, blurring together in countless sights and sounds in a few seconds.

Malone always knew this was a possibility. Go after enough gangs and cartels and eventually this could happen.

There'd been plenty of close calls before, but nothing like this.

"You look like shit, Malone."

Malone recognized the voice.

"You gotta be fuckin' kidding me. Antoine?" Malone said.

"Gotta give you some credit. You ain't as dumb as I thought you were," Antoine said.

"I remembered something you told me. Kings are greedy. Disciples are smart. But you're all a bunch of greedy assholes. And greedy assholes want more territory."

"True," Antoine said with a laugh. "I gotta say, you helped me out a lot. Dropped six Kings for me. Slowing down supply. Drove more business my way. You an old dog, no new tricks. Just had to point you in the right direction."

"What the hell are you talking about?" Malone said.

"About a month ago, I bring a scientist on board. A new way to make product cheaper and speed up production."

"You laced the shit with fentanyl?"

"Hell yeah I did. It's all business, baby. But you've outlived your usefulness now."

"The whole time it was you? You're fucking dead!"

Malone felt a surge of pain as the blowtorch hit his right upper arm.

"No!" he screamed. "Motherfucker!"

"Sorry, you saying something?" Antoine said as he lowered the bandana down from Malone's eyes. "Can't hear what you're saying cause of all that screaming."

Malone squinted from the overhead lights and saw Antoine hold the blowtorch to his arm again.

Malone howled in pain. "I'm gonna rip your fucking head off!"

Antoine laughed. "That shit really don't feel good, huh?"

"Stupid fucker!" Malone screamed.

Antoine smiled. "I'm stupid? That's funny."

"You're fucking dead!"

"Your ass is 'bout to be burnt to a crisp and you making threats?"

"Did I stutter, asshole? You heard me. You're fucking dead."

"Right. Right. I'm gonna miss you man. You been a real help."

"So you'll fucking kill kids and cops just to make more money?"

"Just business, man. Just business."

"You're a greedy piece of dog shit."

"Could say the same thing 'bout you, no? I know you're lining your pockets. Quit acting like it's different. You no better an' me."

"I'm taking crooks and poison off the street."

"You really just putting cops in danger and killing some niggas. You killed Mikey. You earned all this shit."

"Bullshit. I didn't kill Mikey."

"You wouldn't leave him alone. Kept giving him cash. Hell you think he's gonna do? I took his ass to rehab four times. You kept coming back to him, using him over and over again. Your hands ain't clean. They're covered in blood."

"You're just a gaping asshole that's full of shit."

"Keep barking, dog. Your ass is getting put down."

Antoine stepped forward holding the blow torch, then froze in place. He turned off the blow torch, set it down, and reached into his pocket, pulling out his phone.

"Yeah? Shit. Yeah. Be right there." He hung up. "I'm sorry Malone, but I gotta handle some more business. Gonna let my man Ace step in here for a minute. You know Ace, right? Hell, I think he put that hole in your arm," Antoine said.

A young black man with a cursive letter A tattooed on his neck stepped into the room.

"See you, Malone," Antoine said. "Thanks for all you done."

"Fuck off," Malone replied.

"Take your time with this fool," Antoine said to Ace as he left.

"Will do."

Antoine walked out the door.

"You a lucky motherfucker," Ace said.

"If you say so," Malone said with a cough. "I don't feel too lucky."

"Had your ass in my sights. I know I did. Just like the other two fools I smoked."

Malone's face tightened into a scowl. "You know what happens to cop killers?"

Ace laughed. "You mean the ones the cops find. You don't got shit on me," Ace said as he picked up the blowtorch.

"Just planning on lighting me up, huh?"

Ace nodded as he lit the blow torch and stepped closer.

"Wait, wait," Malone said. "Before you get to work on me, can I get a drink?"

Ace stared back at Malone. "Why the hell I do that?"

"I got some cash stashed nearby. Get me a drink, I'll tell you where it is."

Ace put a cigarette in his mouth and lit it with the torch.

"Come on," Malone said. "I saw a few bottles out front. Some whiskey, I think. It's easy money. Whaddya got to lose?"

Ace blew a cloud of smoke in Malone's direction and stared him down. "If you lying, I'm gonna take even more time on you. Find out what your left nut tastes like." Ace stepped out of the backroom and walked into the front.

Malone continued to move his hands to loosen the ropes.

Ace appeared with the bottle in his hand.

"I dunno man, maybe I just keep this shit for myself," Ace said as he took a drink.

Ace held the bottle out and then pulled it back and took another drink and laughed.

"Ain't much left," Ace said. "You got somethin' to tell me, right?"

"Yeah, there's some shit in the trunk. Black Impala. On the street."

Ace held out the bottle in Malone's direction.

"My hands are tied."

"I ain't untying shit." Ace poured the liquor from the bottle and splashed some onto Malone's face, a few drops going into his mouth.

Malone screamed as the liquor burned in his eyes.

"Shit, man," Ace said. "I missed."

"Come on, man. I didn't get any."

Ace poured the whiskey toward Malone's mouth again and he caught it and closed his mouth.

"Okay, motherfucker, say goodbye."

Ace lit the torch again and stepped forward, holding the flame a few inches from Malone's face.

Malone spit out the alcohol causing the flame to spread toward Ace's shirt.

Ace dropped the blowtorch to the floor.

"Goodbye," Malone said with a smile.

"That's it, motherfucker," Ace said as he drew a handgun from his waistband and aimed it at Malone's head.

The door flung open.

Ramirez stormed into the room. "Freeze! Chicago PD!"

Ace turned to fire at Ramirez and was hit with a round to the lower chest. He fell to the floor.

"Shit, Malone," Ramirez said. "You okay?"

"Yeah. You see Antoine leave?"

"No, I didn't see anything."

"Untie me. We gotta find him."

Ramirez pulled out a knife and cut the rope on Malone's wrists.

"Goddamn," Ramirez said, looking at Malone's injured arm. "You sure you're gonna be alright?"

"Yeah. I'll live."

Malone took the bandana from around his neck and wrapped his injured arm. "Holy fucking shit," Malone grimaced.

"You're gonna have to go to the hospital."

"Later."

Malone noticed Ace moving on the floor. "Get his ass in the chair," he said.

Ramirez leaned down and put Ace in the chair.

"Where was Antoine going?" Malone said.

"I ain't sayin' shit," Ace said.

Ace held his hand over his stomach and Malone noticed the blood soaking through his shirt.

"Talk and you go to the hospital," he said. "Say nothing and your ass is gonna bleed out."

"You a fucking asshole."

"Yeah, yeah. What's it gonna be?"

"You ain't got much time man. You wanna live, you better start talking," Ramirez said.

"I ain't no rat," Ace said.

"Yeah, I figured. Real tough guy," Malone said.

Malone picked up the blowtorch off the floor.

"Look," Malone said, "My arm's fucking killing me. I ain't got no problem lighting your ass up."

Malone struggled to light the torch and he turned toward Ramirez and said, "Wanna gimme a hand over here?"

"Yep. It'll be good to get this prick off the street." Ramirez took the lighter from Malone and lit the blowtorch.

Malone pointed it at Ace.

"Shit, I bet this thing could take off that ass ugly ink on your neck."

Malone held the torch to Ace's neck for a brief moment.

Ace howled in pain.

"You ready to talk or you wanting more?" Malone said.

"Scr—screw you."

"I got an idea," Malone said to Ramirez. "Pull his pants down."

Ramirez took a step toward Ace.

"Wait! Wait, man. He's getting a new shipment."

"Where?"

"Navy Pier. 11 tonight."

"What's he driving?

"Chevy SUV. Red."

"There ya go."

Malone hit Ace in the side of the face with the bottom of the blowtorch, knocking him out cold. Malone turned and darted toward the exit with Ramirez behind.

"Wait," Ramirez said. "We can't leave him here like this to bleed out. I gotta call this in."

"Do it in the car," Malone said. "That bastard took out two cops and tried to kill me twice."

"Wait. You need to get to the hospital. That's gotta hurt like hell."

Malone got into his car behind the wheel without replying.

"Hold up. Lemme drive," Ramirez said. "You're in no shape to drive."

"I'm fine."

Ramirez looked back at Malone.

"I'm serious. You need to go to the hospital."

"No, I'm going to go get that fucker."

"You got a plan?"

"Not a plan. An idea."

"What's your idea then?"

"They think I'm dead, and they don't know about you. I wouldn't count us out yet."

Malone drove down East Grand Avenue and slowed the car to a stop by Navy Pier.

"You need some medical attention," Ramirez said.

"This prick ain't getting away. Just take a look around over here. I'll take the east deck."

"You sure?"

"Yeah. I can't do this without you."

"Alright. I'll let you know what I see." Ramirez got out of the car and walked toward the west parking entrance.

Malone continued driving down Grand Avenue, parked around the corner by the east deck, and waited to see if anyone approached on foot or by vehicle. A few minutes later, his phone lit up.

"Nothing going on over here," Ramirez said. "It's empty."

"Okay. Nothing here, either. I'm going inside in a minute. I'll be covering the south and west corners of the deck. Come in from the north entrance."

"Got it."

Malone called Ann, but it went to voicemail. "I'm sorry about all this shit. I'm sorry about everything. I fucked up in so many ways. You'll be able to come back soon."

He put his phone back in his pocket and got out of the car. He slowly walked to the entrance of the parking deck. The pain was getting worse, but Malone used the pain to remind himself that he was still alive.

The deck was mostly empty aside from a dozen or so cars and trucks. He scanned the perimeter, carefully noting the position of each vehicle.

On the opposite side of the parking deck, Malone saw two men standing behind a white van. He hid behind a nearby concrete column and watched.

One smoked a cigarette and the other leaned against the van's bumper.

After making sure it was clear, Malone came out into the open but stayed low and used nearby vehicles for cover. He crouched down next to a grey Civic and heard the sound of another vehicle pull into the deck behind him. He squeezed under the car nearby, staying out of sight.

The incoming vehicle was a red Chevrolet SUV with tinted windows. Malone watched as the SUV parked behind the white van. He immediately recognized the driver as Antoine. In the passenger seat was a large man named Peewee, muscle for the Gangster Disciples. Antoine and Peewee got out of the vehicle. Malone noticed that Peewee was holding a large black bag.

Malone called Ramirez. "Got activity on the west end," he whispered. "White van is cartel, red SUV is Gangster Disciples."

"Okay, be right there."

"Hurry."

Malone took a deep breath and steadied himself. He felt the pain come to the surface. He knew he was moving slower than usual, but knew the adrenaline would help him surge forward. He focused his thoughts to block out the distraction. After a couple more deep breaths, he crouched between two cars and moved toward the white van and red SUV. Now he was within firing distance. He heard the voices but couldn't make out the words.

Malone shifted his eyes toward the stairwell, watching for Ramirez. He drew his P226, aimed it toward the four men, then quickly looked back toward the stairwell just in time to see Ramirez appear on the stairway.

Malone moved forward. "CPD—freeze!" he barked. "Don't fucking move! Put your hands up!"

The four men scattered. One opened the back door to the van and took cover inside.

Malone fired a couple of rounds and hit the van's back window, shattering the glass.

Antoine darted back toward the red SUV.

Ramirez fired a few shots into the side of the van.

"Freeze, asshole!" Ramirez yelled.

The gunfire stopped and all was silent. A long series of shots from an AK47 rang out from the back of the white van, causing Malone and Ramirez to duck down.

Malone was down on hands and knees by a car while he waited for a break in gunfire. When it stopped, Malone popped up and fired a few rounds at the van.

Ramirez emptied his Glock on the gunman. Ramirez watched him fall forward onto the concrete, no movement.

The other man disappeared into the back of the van and resurfaced with another AK47. He fired at Ramirez and hit him in the chest.

Ramirez was on the ground and not moving.

Malone immediately fired back and shot the man in the chest repeatedly. Malone saw the passenger door of the red SUV swing open.

Peewee came out with a pistol in his right hand.

"Freeze, asshole! Drop it!" Malone screamed.

Peewee looked toward Malone's direction and set the gun on the ground and put his hands on his head.

"Don't fucking move," Malone said, stumbling to his feet and stepping forward. "It's over." Malone heard footsteps from behind, then was hit in the back. He fell down to the ground, opened his eyes and saw his P226 a couple feet from him on the ground under a car.

"Ya like that bullet in your back, mothafucka?" Peewee said as he picked up his gun again and walked toward Malone and kicked him in the side.

Malone held in his urge to groan and laid there motion-less. "Little man here just capped your sorry ass."

Peewee nodded toward a young black teenager, barely old enough to drive, holding a handgun. Peewee towered over Malone's body and kicked him in the gut. "Don't pass out yet," Peewee said. "You're gonna have to look at me before you die, mothafucka. I wanna tell you somethin.' We own this town. And you ain't gonna be slowin' us down no more."

He kicked Malone in the side a few more times.

Malone rolled over, reaching toward his stomach.

"Look at me, motherfucker! Fucking look at me!" Peewee screamed in Malone's face.

Malone opened his eyes. "I am, asshole," Malone said as he fired his backup pistol at Peewee. A shot went through his jaw and jerked his head back as blood splashed out the other side. Malone turned quickly to his right, firing a burst at the teen's kneecap, dropping him to the ground.

The teen shrieked in pain.

Malone growled as he cradled his injured arm on the ground.

"Don't feel too good, does it?" Malone slowly tried to get back up to his feet and fell back down. "Fucking shit," he said. He slowly got back up. He heard the SUV's engine start, then the tires squealed as it rounded a corner toward the exit. Malone awkwardly limped as fast as he could to catch the SUV before it left.

The SUV rounded the corner.

Malone stepped into its path, firing at the windshield. The SUV swerved, lost control, and hit a concrete column.

Malone limped toward the vehicle as smoke rose from under the hood.

Antoine was still in the driver's seat.

Malone pulled a clip out of his vest and reloaded his gun. "Freeze! Put your fucking hands up!"

Antoine's face was bloody, and he wasn't moving.

Malone kept his gun aimed for a few more seconds. Still no movement.

Antoine opened his eyes and fired a burst from his Glock, hitting Malone in the chest and sending him to the ground.

Malone was completely still.

Antoine tumbled out of the driver's side and limped away.

Malone slowly leaned forward and steadied himself as he got up to his feet.

Antoine collapsed on his way to the exit and got back up.

Malone saw Antoine running away and said, "Drop it, asshole." Malone aimed his gun at Antoine. "It's over."

Antoine tucked the Glock into his pants and held hands up over his head. "No, it ain't motherfucker," he said. "Not even close. You're ain't gonna win, you dumb fuck. You're never gonna..."

Antoine lowered his arms and spun around with the Glock drawn in his right hand. Malone fired a shot into Antoine's forehead and watched his body fall to the ground.

"Why don't you shut the fuck up." Malone coughed and started to spit up blood. He slipped his hand underneath his body armor. Blood covered his fingertips. He took several wobbly steps and collapsed on the ground.

His thoughts started to drift and blur together as his eyes gazed into the lights of the Chicago skyline.

Ann.

James.

Max.

Leo.

Johnny.

Mikey.

Sarah.

Andrew.

Malone continued to lie still on the ground as blood

slowly pooled around him. He looked up briefly and saw Ramirez crouched over him.

"I thought—you were a goner."

"Naw. Vest caught it. I'll be sore as hell later, but I'm still here."

"Good," Malone said. He felt a sense of peace come over him. It was over. A slight smile came to his face.

"Hey. Are you smiling here?" Ramirez said.

"Yeah, maybe a little," Malone whispered.

Malone shut his eyes as the sound of sirens swelled in the night.

THE STORY CONTINUES...

There's more to this story. A lot more. This novel is just one piece of a bigger puzzle. And I'd like to share with you more pieces of that puzzle.

Just visit **authorjimwoods.com/free-stories/** to receive some more stories.

ABOUT THE AUTHOR

Jim Woods is a writer from Akron, Ohio. Once upon a time, he wanted to become an FBI agent because of Fox Mulder on the X-Files. Sadly, that never happened because the X-Files don't really exist. And that is why Jim writes fiction today. You can connect with Jim at www.authorjimwoods.com